D0210830

ALFRED A. KNOPF
1915 · 100 YEARS · 2015

ALSO BY MICHAEL HARVEY

The Innocence Game

We All Fall Down

The Third Rail

The Fifth Floor

The Chicago Way

THE GOVERNOR'S WIFE

THE GOVERNOR'S WIFE

Michael Harvey

Alfred A. Knopf New York 2015

THIS IS A BORZOI BOOK
PUBLISHED BY ALFRED A. KNOPF

www.aaknopf.com

Library of Congress Cataloging-in-Publication Data
Harvey, Michael T.
The governor's wife / by Michael Harvey. — First edition.
pages cm
ISBN 978-0-307-95864-8 (hardcover)
ISBN 978-0-307-95865-5 (eBook)
1. Private investigators—Fiction. 2. Political corruption—Fiction. 3. Chicago (Ill.)—Fiction. I. Title.
PS3608.A78917G68 2015
813'.6—dc23 2014014535

Jacket image composite: Angela Butler Photography / Getty Images; David Henderson / OJO Images / Getty Images
Jacket design by Oliver Munday

Manufactured in the United States of America
First Edition

For my mom and dad

THE GOVERNOR'S WIFE

CHAPTER 1

My laptop is set up so a tiny black box flashes in the corner of the screen every time I get an e-mail. The alerts arrive like an endless parade of crows, pecking away at me with people I don't want to talk to and problems I'd rather ignore. I don't know how my Mac got programmed to do this and have no idea how to stop it. So I live with my birds. The one that hired me fluttered in at 2:14 p.m. on a Tuesday afternoon. I took one look at the subject line and clicked through to read the rest.

Mr. Kelly,

Would like to retain you to find Raymond Perry. Use any and all means at your disposal to accomplish same. Global search okay. Money, no object. If you are willing to take the job, please hit reply to this message. A $100,000 retainer will be wired into an account set up for you. Another $100,000 will be wired when you locate Mr. Perry. A separate fund for expenses will also be established and replenished as needed. Details on accounts, etc., will be forwarded upon acceptance of the terms of employment.

I'm sure there's a manual somewhere that sets out the guidelines for when and how private investigators should take on new cases. Knowing the name of your client would seem to be a necessity. When the proposed retainer hits six figures, however, necessity becomes a somewhat elastic concept, and guidelines tend to get tossed out the window. Be that as it may, the money wasn't what did it for me. Don't get me wrong. The cash caught my eye. In fact, there might have been a moment or two of involuntary drool at the prospect of two hundred K sitting in a bank account with my name on it. But the reason I hit REPLY was not the money. Really. It was the name. Raymond Perry. As I waited for my newest client to get back to me with particulars such as account numbers and wiring instructions, I plugged Perry's name into Google. I knew the story. Hell, everyone knew the story. Still, it made for good reading. I brewed myself a pot of coffee and caught up on Illinois's former governor and convicted felon. I started with the FBI's "Most Wanted" list and Perry's mug shot residing, as it had been for the past year and a half, in slot number one.

CHAPTER 2

There were more than five thousand articles on Raymond Perry's sentencing hearing. The *New York Times* did a tick tock of the day that ran four pages in one of its Sunday editions. It even had video clips and still photos of Perry culled from the day's coverage. I pulled up the piece and started to read. On February 15, 2012, Raymond Perry and his wife, Marie, left their house at 7:37 a.m. Media choppers followed them from their home in Winnetka, all the way down the Edens and into the Loop. Perry's black Caddy pulled up in front of the Dearborn entrance to the Dirksen Federal Building at 8:29. I clicked on a video clip labeled PERRY ARRIVAL. The press was corralled behind steel barricades set up on either side of a pair of revolving doors. Camera shutters snapped and questions flew as Perry helped his wife out of the backseat. The former governor navigated the thirty feet of pavement like a seasoned pro—head high, left hand holding his wife's, right hand extended in a small wave to a woman who carried a YOU'RE STILL OUR GOVERNOR sign and bobbed up and down with the boundless excitement that could only have come from living in downstate Illinois. Perry pushed through the doors at 8:33 a.m. I clicked on a second clip that picked him up as he ran another gauntlet of cameras in the lobby. Reporters continued to yell questions, but Perry kept his head down and made straight for a set of security scanners. He talked with his attorney, Kenneth Krebs, as they waited at the metal detector, then beelined for a bank of elevators. Perry hit the elevators at 8:41. His wife was never more than five feet from his side.

I rewound the clip and watched it a second time. Then I went back to the article. Perry took the elevator up twenty-five floors to courtroom number 2503, home of the honorable James J. Hogan. Four months earlier, Perry had been convicted in the same courtroom on seventeen counts of wire fraud and racketeering. Like any red-blooded Chicago politician, Perry had only done what came naturally. He'd met with potential donors and threatened to destroy them unless they ponied up enough dough for his reelection run. Not a big deal, except the feds were listening, and Perry didn't pull any punches when it came to his lust for campaign cash. The trial lasted almost a month, but it was really all over once the government played its first recording. It's not that Chicagoans were especially bothered by the idea of a politician lining his pockets. They just didn't appreciate having their civic face rubbed in it.

According to the *Times* log, Perry walked into Hogan's courtroom at 8:47. Hogan called proceedings to order at just after nine. The hearing dragged on for almost three hours. After lunch, the judge asked Perry if he wanted to speak. He declined. Hogan grunted and moved on to sentencing. The long-faced Irishman gave Perry thirty-seven years in the federal pen, with a minimum of thirty years to be served before any possible parole. As the sentence was read, Marie Perry sat pale and perfect on a bench behind her husband. Krebs tugged at his client's elbow and whispered in his ear. Perry listened and frowned. Otherwise, the former governor was stoic. He nodded toward Hogan as the judge left the bench. Then Perry shrugged on his coat and walked out of the courtroom. It was just two in the afternoon.

There were maybe fifty people milling around in the corridor when Perry made his exit. The press was generally prohibited from taking photos or asking questions outside the courtrooms, so most of the reporters had already scurried downstairs to get going on their stories or set up for an exit shot. Perry talked privately with his attorney for approximately ten minutes. According to the *Times,* the two stood close together, foreheads nearly touching. At one point, Krebs gripped his client's shoulder and Perry nodded slowly. When they'd finished, he clapped Krebs on the back and found his wife's hand. They walked down a long marble hallway, toward an area the bailiffs had cordoned off. The former governor stopped at the velvet rope and turned, a half smile playing across his lips. An AP photographer managed to sneak a single shot—Ray Perry's *Mona Lisa* moment as the world crashed down around him. It was a photo that would threaten to melt the Internet in the hours and days that followed.

Just beyond the velvet rope and around a corner was an elevator that ran all the way to the basement parking garage. Marie Perry pressed the DOWN button, and the arrow above the door lit up almost immediately. That was when Ray told his wife he had to go to the men's room. Marie said she'd wait. Ray insisted she go on ahead. According to Marie Perry, her husband said he wanted "a moment alone." There was no one close enough to hear the Perrys as they called for their elevator. There was, however, a set of security cameras. And the *Times* had gained access to them.

I punched up a file labeled DIRKSEN SECURITY FOOTAGE. The first image was of Perry and his wife, standing in the hallway. The second picture showed Marie stepping into the elevator. Then came a series of still shots. Perry heading into the men's room, time stamped 2:24 p.m. Perry coming out of the men's room, time stamped 2:36. Perry standing in front of the elevators, glancing up at the camera. Perry getting on the elevator himself.

I knew how the tale ended, but read the rest of the *Times* article anyway. The elevator car that stopped on the twenty-fifth floor to pick up Ray Perry had one passenger in it: a journeyman electrician named Eddie Ward. Eddie was in the federal building that morning to do some work on the twenty-seventh floor and was en route to the thirteenth to check out a relay switch. There were no cameras inside the cars, but footage from another hallway camera showed Ward, Cubs hat on and a canvas tool bag slung over his shoulder, getting off on the thirteenth. The elevator then proceeded, nonstop, to the garage level. Perry's wife was waiting when the elevator doors opened. The car, however, was empty.

It took a couple of minutes for Marie Perry to realize what was happening. At 2:43 p.m., she called her husband's cell phone. It went to voice mail. Marie called Krebs at 2:45. He came down to the garage, accompanied by three state police officers. At 2:52 a call went out to secure all exits to the building, and police began a floor-by-floor search. When the Canine Unit showed up, the media began to stir. Within a half hour, the place went up for grabs.

CNN broke the story at 3:35 that afternoon. As police scurried to and fro behind her, a blond reporter named Whitney Wild stood in the lobby of the federal building and told the country about the rumors starting to swirl. First, it was that Perry had taken ill. Then, he'd tried to take his own life. Finally, the truth. Illinois's disgraced, impeached, and convicted felon of a governor had taken a powder—disappeared without a trace. Investigators would later speculate that an access panel in the roof of the elevator car might have been breached. Every door or hallway that would have gotten Perry out of the elevator shaft, however, was covered by a camera. Perry never appeared on any of the footage. He'd simply vanished.

I closed up the *Times* article and looked out the window. It was late in the afternoon and the traffic on Broadway was light. The sun was low in the sky and mellow, spreading itself over the North Side like a soft cloak of spun gold. I pulled a worn copy of Ovid's *Metamorphoses* from the side drawer of my desk and leafed through it until I found the story of Daedalus and Icarus. A master craftsman, Daedalus had fashioned wings for his son out of feathers and wax, then taught him to fly. Icarus, however, ignored his father's warning to navigate a middle course. Instead, he set out to touch the sun.

. . . Icarus began to feel the joy
Of beating wings in air and steered his course
Beyond his father's lead: all the wide sky
Was there to tempt him as he steered toward heaven.
Meanwhile the heat of sun struck at his back
And where his wings were joined, sweet-smelling
fluid
Ran hot that once was wax. His naked arms
Whirled into wind; his lips, still calling out
His father's name, were gulfed in the dark sea.

I closed the book and thought about Ray Perry. An unknown when he ran for governor, his campaign had been electrifying; his rise, meteoric. The downfall, when it happened, seemed more inevitable than tragic. Too much, too soon never worked very well, especially in Chicago. My laptop beeped once. I looked over at the screen. Another black bird had arrived. This one carried a hundred thousand dollars in its beak—an offering from my newest client, still without a name. I knew that should bother me, and knew I'd probably regret the fact that it didn't. For now, however, there was work to be done. And a modern-day Icarus to be fished out of the drink.

CHAPTER 3

I walked to the front of James Hogan's courtroom and took a seat at one of the counsel tables. The room was empty and still. The walls were covered in book-matched, black-walnut paneling that soaked up light like a fresh coat of polish. Hogan's bench stood in front of me—a towering tribute to mahogany topped by a thick leather chair with a stub of a microphone before it. The effect was meant to intimidate. From where I sat, mission accomplished.

I left the courtroom and made my way toward the elevators Perry had used on the day he disappeared. There was one security camera covering the area. I stuck my head in the men's room. Three stalls, three urinals, and a couple of sinks that reminded me of third grade. The ceilings were at least eleven feet high and looked to be made of solid drywall. No cameras. No windows. I went back outside and took an elevator to the twenty-seventh floor. According to the building's directory, most of the space on this floor was taken up by judges' chambers and various administrative offices. I'd done a little digging and discovered that Eddie Ward had been working on an electrical problem caused by a vending machine located somewhere on twenty-seven. I walked the floor looking for the machine, but couldn't find it. I was sitting on a bench in the hallway, wondering how many Eddie Wards there might be in the Chicagoland area, when a man in his early thirties wandered around the corner and sat down on the floor. He took out a sketchbook and began to draw.

"Hey," I said.

The man's shoulders jumped and the sketchbook snapped shut. "Sorry. I didn't see you there."

"What are you doing?"

He pointed to the ceiling. "Mies van der Rohe."

"Uh-huh."

"You know Mies?"

"I've heard of him."

The man pulled himself up and walked over to where I sat. He was clean shaven with light, clean features, broad shoulders, and thick arms and wrists. He wore faded blue jeans, a button-down blue oxford, and rumpled black sport coat. Along with the sketchbook, he carried a camera bag that he kept next to him as he took a seat on the bench.

"My name's Andrew Wallace."

"Hi, Andrew. Michael Kelly."

Wallace opened up the sketchbook and laid it over his knees. "I'm sketching some of the period details in the courtrooms and hallways." Wallace pointed to a pencil drawing and then toward the ceiling. "The crown moldings here are quite distinctive. Simple, elegant, strong. Reflects the exterior design of the building. Classic Mies."

"Where do you go to school, Andrew?"

"The Art Institute. Getting a master's in urban architecture. I'm a bit of a Chicago buff."

"Me too."

"Really?"

"Sure. Let me ask you something, how well do you know this building?"

Wallace glanced around with sudden suspicion. "How well do I *know* it?"

"How well do you know your way around?"

"Oh. Pretty well." Wallace touched his camera bag. "Taking pictures. Doing my sketches."

"You know if there's a vending machine up here?"

The grad student cocked his head like he'd heard wrong. "Excuse me?"

"A vending machine. On this floor."

"There used to be a Dippin' Dots."

"Dippin' Dots?"

"Freeze-dried ice cream. You never had Dippin' Dots?"

"Never had Dippin' Dots."

"They took the machine out about a year ago. It was just down the hall."

"Could you show me?"

Wallace led me down one corridor, then a second. He stopped at a small, empty alcove. "It was in here. I heard one of the judges liked his ice cream and had it put in."

"You say they took it out about a year ago?"

"In May or April. I thought it was kind of weird to have it up here. They don't have machines on the other floors. Just downstairs near the café."

"No kidding. Who took the machine out?"

"No idea. Why?"

I shook my head. "Never mind."

"There's another one in the basement."

"Another Dippin' Dots?"

"Yes."

"Can I get down there?"

"No, but I could."

I smiled. "Lead on."

. . .

Andrew Wallace pulled out a laminated card he kept on a chain around his neck and slid it through a reader. Then he pressed a button and our elevator began to drop.

"They gave you an access pass for the building?" I said.

"Just the garage and a few restricted areas. I'm here all the time anyway."

"For the Mies project?"

"My thesis."

"Right." I stared at a run of floor numbers as they lit up above the door. Beside me Wallace shifted his feet and cleared his throat. I glanced over. Mistake.

"Are you a cop?" he said.

"I'm a private investigator."

"I knew it. So why are you here?"

"I'm working a case, but I can't tell you much about it."

"Is it a murder?"

"That's a pretty good question."

"And you can't answer it?"

"Probably not." Our elevator slowed, then stopped. The doors eased open. "You still gonna show me our ice-cream machine?"

Wallace adjusted the camera bag on his shoulder. "This way."

We walked into a space full of strained light and thick shadows. I stopped for a moment and took a couple of pictures of the elevator with my phone. Then I took a shot of the security camera covering the elevator and a shot of the garage. Wallace led me through a maze of cars and empty parking spaces until we reached a small door.

"This is where a lot of the cleaning and maintenance guys keep their lockers." Wallace pointed just ahead. "There's the machine."

The Dippin' Dots machine was massive and blue, with red and green balloons plastered all over it. An Illinois state vending permit was stuck just above the face of a grinning clown. The machine was licensed to a corporation named Double D Entertainment, Inc. I wrote down the name in a small black notebook.

"Damn." Wallace gave the machine a halfhearted kick.

"What?"

He pointed to a flashing red light and the words SOLD OUT glowing in neon-green type.

"Guess they don't keep the thing stocked up," I said.

"Like everything else," Wallace said.

"You want to head back up?"

"That's it?"

"Not very exciting, is it?"

"Why do you care about the Dippin' Dots machine?"

"I don't care about the machine. Just its owner."

"Oh."

We walked back through the garage and waited for the elevator. Wallace took out his camera and began to scroll through some photos he'd shot.

"What do you do with the pictures?" I said.

"They're part of my research. Over the last four years I've taken thousands of photos in the Loop. Hell, I've probably taken a few thousand inside this building alone."

Our elevator arrived with a soft chime. We got on, and the car began to climb.

"You've been shooting in here for the last four years?" I said.

"Between undergrad and graduate school, pretty much."

"How about trials, stuff like that?"

"You mean do I have access not granted to the regular media?"

"That's exactly what I mean."

We arrived at the twenty-fifth floor. There were a few people hanging around in front of Hogan's courtroom. I gave them a wide berth and found a quiet corner where we could sit. Wallace kept his camera bag beside him as he spoke.

"What is it you're looking for, Mr. Kelly?"

"Do you have access?"

"I never got into a courtroom if that's what you're after."

"It's not."

The grad student licked his lips. Now that we'd come to it, maybe he didn't want to play detective so much. "They let me take photos in some restricted areas as long as I'm discreet. Mostly hallway stuff during some of the trials."

"So you might be able to help me?"

"Depends on what you're looking for."

"The Perry trial."

Wallace nodded like he'd known all along. "You mean the day he disappeared."

"Were you here?"

"I shot a few things. Nothing too exciting."

"Where were you?"

Wallace pointed down the hall. "I was by the elevators. The governor and his wife walked around the corner, and she hit the call button. I snapped off a few pictures while they were waiting."

"Did you see Perry himself get on the elevator?"

"Actually, no. He went into the bathroom and I rode one of the cars down."

"So you followed Ms. Perry to the garage?"

"Yes. I thought I could get some shots of them driving out. Of course, the governor never showed."

"Anyone ever look at your pictures?"

"Security grabbed them after everything happened. Then I had to talk to a bunch of federal investigators. Guys like you."

"Hardly."

"Well, there wasn't much to tell them. We went over each photo and then they let me go."

"Do you still have the shots?"

"Not with me but, yeah, I still have them."

"Do the feds know you have them?"

"They told me if anything showed up in the media they'd find me and arrest me. I asked them for what, and they told me they'd think of something."

"They would." I took out a couple of business cards. "Keep one of these for yourself. Write your contact info on the other."

Wallace wrote down a cell number and e-mail on the back of one of the cards and tucked the other in his jacket pocket. "You want to take a look at my photos?"

"I want to buy them."

"They're not gonna be much help."

"Let me be the judge of that."

"I have to work all day tomorrow and the next."

"Can you e-mail them to me?"

"To be honest, I'd rather show you. Otherwise, I'm not sure you'd know what you were looking at."

"How about you call me when you get free and we'll figure out a time to meet?"

"Sounds good." Wallace got up to go and paused.

"What is it?" I said.

"Did you know the Perrys?"

"I met the governor once or twice. Why?"

"His wife."

"What about her?"

"She seemed a little out of it that day."

"Her husband was going off to jail for thirty years."

"Yeah, I guess. Tell you the truth she kind of creeped me out."

"Call me, Andrew."

"Cool."

I watched as the grad student disappeared around a corner. Then I took out my smartphone and pulled up the website for the Illinois Secretary of State. I accessed its corporate records division and plugged in DOUBLE D ENTERTAINMENT. The corporation was no longer in good standing in Illinois. Its registered agent was a man named Paul Goggin. I did a quick wire search for Goggin and came up with nothing. I found one cell number for a "Paul Goggin" in an online directory, but no address. When I dialed the number, it was disconnected. I logged off and watched people go in and out of Hogan's courtroom. The place looked like it was filling up. I walked down the hallway to the elevator Ray Perry had taken and rode it to the ground floor. The car was like a million others. Four walls, a floor, and ceiling. I took a couple of photos of the interior, then glanced up at the emergency exit cut into the roof. I took a picture of that as well. The elevator pinged and the door opened. I walked through the lobby of the federal building, hit the revolving doors, and pushed my way into the Loop.

CHAPTER 4

I wrangled Eddie Ward's address and number from a producer I knew over at CBS. She told me she'd been trying to get an interview with him for the past six months, but no one ever answered his phone. Of course, she'd never bothered to drive out to the address. Maybe she thought Eddie would wander in on his own, looking to give her an exclusive.

The electrician lived on the top floor of a skinny three-flat just west of Palmer Square. I got there around eleven and knocked on his door, but there was no answer. I made as much noise as I could coming back down the stairs and stopped in front of the second-floor apartment. I knew she was looking at me through the peephole and waited. My patience was rewarded as the door creaked open and a nose poked out.

"Beatrice Sanderson?"

"How do you know my name?"

"I saw it on the buzzer."

"What do you want?"

"I was looking for Eddie Ward."

The door opened another inch. The nose was attached to a woman who looked more like a squirrel—the twitching, sniffing, inquisitive kind. Harmless enough . . . and hunting for nuts.

"He's long gone," she said.

"You don't say."

"Hasn't been around for months."

"That unusual for Eddie?"

"Highly."

"Not likely to go off to Vegas?"

"Eddie?" Beatrice thought that was pretty damn funny. "You a friend?"

"Business." I had my gun on my hip. She went from that to my face and came up with "cop." I was more than happy to let her think that, especially since I was about to engage in some breaking and entering.

"Listen, I need to get into Eddie's place."

"I don't have a key." Beatrice opened the door wider to let me in. Stale air and old age had made their bed in there and weren't leaving any time soon. At least not until death came along and put them out of a job.

"I'll take your word for it," I said. "I might have to force the door a bit up there. Might make some noise."

"No one lives on the first floor. Just me and Eddie. Or used to be Eddie."

"So you don't mind if I bang around a little?"

"Gonna rob the place?"

"No, ma'am."

A wave of her hand. "Knock yourself out."

"You won't call the police?"

"Why would I do that?" She nodded at my gun. "Got 'em right here."

I walked back upstairs and considered the door to Eddie's apartment. Then I planted a size ten just under the lock. The jamb burst in a splinter of nails and wood. And I was in. The place was a cheap one-bedroom that felt like it hadn't been lived in for a while. I noticed a fine layer of dust on the vinyl couch and a residue of grit that crunched under my shoes. I stuck my head in the bedroom. Eddie's bed was made and his room was neat. I looked in the bathroom and saw nothing but a closed shower curtain. Eddie had a couple of paperback books on a shelf in the living room and a small table with a drawer full of old bills. I poked around, looking for something personal. Photos, a day planner, checkbook. There was nothing. I took another look at the bills. The latest was a past-due gas notice from four months ago. I went into the kitchenette and checked the stove. Working. I swept up some of the grit off the floor and slipped it into a Baggie. Then I did the same with the dust on the couch. I closed up the door as best I could and walked back downstairs. Beatrice was waiting.

"Made enough noise."

"Sorry."

"Don't bother me none."

"You haven't seen Eddie in a few months?"

"Already told you that."

"How about his mail? Who takes that?"

"There was a pile." The old woman shifted her weight in the door. I could see a tray with her breakfast still on it, set up in front of a TV. Dr. Phil was on, talking to a woman about her fear of wearing red.

"What happened to it?" I said.

"Mailman took it away."

I refused to believe Beatrice hadn't gotten to the bottom of that. I wasn't disappointed.

"He told me they'd gotten a termination notice."

"You mean a forwarding address?"

"That's what I said. The mailman told me it's different. With a termination notice the post office just collects the mail until the person has a fixed address."

"This was a few weeks ago?"

"At least a month. Maybe more." Her eyes rolled toward the ceiling. "Is Eddie dead up there?"

"I didn't see him."

Beatrice seemed a little disappointed. "I've got to go. Do you have a card?"

I gave her one. She tucked it into the pocket of her robe without looking at it and shut the door in my face.

CHAPTER 5

Marie Perry maintained a suite of offices on Michigan Avenue, south of the river and just north of the Art Institute. The reception area featured floor-to-ceiling windows overlooking Millennium Park. The receptionist, a matchstick of a woman dressed in black from head to toe, had already offered me fourteen different flavors of herbal tea. I told her I was fine. Then she brought out a selection of apples from six different states. Again, I took a pass. Finally, she told me they were having a yoga class for everyone in the office at one. They had spare workout clothes, towels, and a mat if I was interested. I showed her my gun and told her I had some people to shoot later on and wanted to keep my edge. The receptionist pretty much left me alone after that.

I'd sat there maybe fifteen minutes when a second woman, also malnourished and swaddled in black, came out to get me. She walked me down a hall filled with bright colors and a soft hissing that sounded like steam escaping from a busted pipe.

"What's that?" I said.

"What?"

"Sounds like a gas leak."

"Oh." The assistant looked back at me with that zombie/acolyte smile you used to see only at an *Oprah* taping. "That's their waterfall. Isn't it beautiful?"

"Whose waterfall?"

"Marie and Ray's. They spent a month in Kenya. Marie recorded all the sounds of their trip so they could reconnect with Africa whenever they felt the need. These are the waterfalls of Thika. I'm thinking of playing it at my wedding once I get engaged. Course I have to get a boyfriend first. Here we are."

The assistant pushed open a door and I walked into Marie Perry's office. In case I had any doubts, there was a life-size portrait of her and Ray hung on the wall directly above her chair. The shot was taken at least five years and half a lifetime ago. Ray was dressed in a tux and reaching out to shake a hand. Marie Perry was glammed up in an evening gown and glancing over her bare shoulder at the world she'd left behind.

"That's a Bichet."

I turned. The woman herself stood in the doorway.

"The gown, I mean. Andre Bichet. The photograph was taken by Bellows. He used to take all our shots when . . . well, you know when. I keep it around to impress I'm not sure who these days."

Marie Perry walked behind her desk. She was dressed in faded jeans and an oversize sweater with a set of reading glasses stuck up on her forehead. Back in the day, she'd been touted as the engine that powered the Raymond Perry political machine. She knew who to woo and who to avoid. More important, she wasn't afraid to stick a knife in someone's back if she had to. And in Chicago, you always had to.

Most people assumed the governor's mansion in Springfield was just the beginning for Marie Perry. The woman had plans. A seat in the U.S. Senate for her husband, maybe a run for the White House if the cards fell right. But first lady of Illinois was as far as she'd rise. And it had been a costly climb.

The years had done their best work on her face. Puffiness around the lips and eyes. A loose bag of skin under the chin. Lines carved into pale, drawn cheeks. Marie Perry was decaying before my very eyes. Even worse, she was being mocked by the polished image that hung just behind her.

"You mind if I smoke?" she said and sat down.

"What about your yoga class?"

She chuckled and pulled out a pack of Marlboros. "I gave that up a while back. You want one?"

I shook my head and took a seat across from her. Marie lit up and streamed smoke from the side of her mouth. It wreathed her head, then floated toward the ceiling.

"I used to do yoga, meditation, chanting. The whole nine yards. Then Ray disappeared, the feds arrested me, and the press had me for breakfast, lunch, and dinner. Walk through that shit storm and tell me how *nama*-fucking-*ste* life sounds."

I was going to ask about Kenya and the waterfalls but figured no one should have too much fun in one day.

"You told my assistant you wanted to talk about Ray," Marie said, playing with the pack of Marlboros as she spoke.

"I'm a private investigator."

"I know who you are, Mr. Kelly. Why are you interested in my husband?"

"You mean who hired me?"

She ashed her cigarette and drew one foot up onto her chair. "Exactly. Who hired you? And why do they care about Ray?"

"I don't know the answers to either of those questions."

"And yet you took the job anyway. Must be a good bit of money."

"It's not about the money."

Smoke bubbled out of her mouth along with the laughter. "Don't bullshit me and I'll extend you the same courtesy."

"Can we talk about your husband?"

"Why should we?"

"I don't know. Why did you agree to meet today?"

"Maybe I was bored. Not a lot of demand these days for a disgraced former first lady, especially one half the world thinks helped engineer her husband's disappearance. The only people I talk to on a regular basis are the feds. Believe it or not, I almost look forward to that monthly colonoscopy."

"Why did Ray do it?"

"He was looking at thirty years in prison."

"Any other reason?"

"My husband didn't tell me about his little plan, if that's what you're asking."

There was a knock on the door, and the assistant stuck her head in. "Your appointment's in half an hour."

"Thank you, Pamela. I'll just be a few minutes."

Marie Perry gave Pamela a withering smile and waited until she'd shut the door. "They're all interns. Too naïve to realize I'm nothing. So we pretend I'm still first lady. And I go to third-rate fund-raisers and ribbon cuttings. Today it's a cupcake shop in Andersonville. They pay for my time. Sad thing is I'd probably do it for free."

"Let's get back to Ray."

"Ray's gone, Mr. Kelly. And he's not coming back." She crushed her cigarette into an ashtray and pivoted in her chair to look out a window, at the front steps of the Art Institute. I noticed a slight tremor in her hands as she steepled them under her chin.

"Ms. Perry?"

"Yes?"

"Are you all right?"

She turned her head and pinned me to the wall with a bloodless stare any self-respecting corpse would have been proud of. "You're the private investigator, Mr. Kelly. What do you think?"

CHAPTER 6

I walked down Michigan Avenue, trying to shake off the uncomfortable feeling that Marie Perry drank a couple of pints of blood for dinner every night and crawled into a coffin when she needed some shut-eye. I stopped at an afterthought of a bar on the corner of Michigan and Monroe and ordered a Jim Beam, rocks. My phone buzzed and I ignored it. Then I punched in a number and waited.

"Kelly?"

"Vince, what's up?"

Vince Rodriguez was a homicide detective with the Chicago PD. He was also a friend. It wasn't like I had a lot of friends. Some of that was by design. The rest just came naturally. Rodriguez, however, was a constant. Someone I could count on even when it wasn't in his best interest . . . which was often.

"Where you been hiding?"

"Laying low. Working." I hadn't talked to Rodriguez in three months. I hadn't talked to anyone significant in three months. Except for my dog. And I was pretty sure she was getting sick of my act as well. "What's been going on?"

"Same old bullshit. Still dealing with the West Side. People hate the cops, lining up to file their lawsuits. Lawyers running around with their hands out."

It had been four years since the West Side had been the target of a bioweapons attack. Five hundred people had died and Chicago still hadn't fully recovered. Physically, emotionally, or psychologically. The city would survive. A little scratched and dented maybe, but that was Chicago. Algren put it best—"like loving a woman with a broken nose."

"You got a little time to talk?" I said.

"Go ahead."

"Not on the phone."

"Goddamnit, Kelly."

"It's nothing. Just a conversation. One drink and a conversation. You'll like it."

"I won't like it." A pause. "Where are you?"

I told him. Fifteen minutes later, the cop slid onto a stool and signaled for the bartender.

"What are you drinking?"

"Beam, rocks."

The detective nodded. "Same."

The bartender went off to pour Rodriguez's drink. He pointed his chin at a TV hung from the ceiling. "You see the news yet?"

"No. Why?"

"We found an infant up in Lincoln Park this morning." The bartender returned with the drink. Rodriguez took a sip and sighed. "Damn, that's good."

"What's it about?"

"Someone told us they saw this guy leave a baby in the trunk of a car. I happened to be nearby and rolled on it. Turns out the car was using phony plates and had been stolen in Toronto."

"And the kid?"

"Who knows? Could be just some lousy parents who like to steal cars. Could be they were looking to sell the kid."

"Black market?"

"We're seeing a lot more of it. Word is they might be running an operation out of Chicago. Anyway, the kid was cute as hell. Latino. A news crew got a shot of him as we pulled him out of the trunk. Bingo. Fucking story blows up. All of a sudden I got five cameras looking for another shot of the kid. We shipped him off to the NICU at Northwestern Memorial, then held a press conference." Rodriguez rattled the ice cubes in his glass and studied me under the barroom light. "You all right?"

"Never better."

"Have you seen her?"

"Seen who?"

Rodriguez shook his head and glanced again at the TV. "Hey, can you put on the news? WGN."

The bartender came over with a remote and changed the channel.

"Thanks." Rodriguez turned back to me. "You want to talk? Or you just gonna stew in it?"

"It" was a woman named Rachel Swenson. She was a federal judge and had been my girlfriend until she sold me out to the feds. We'd tried to put it back together a couple of times over the past year and almost got there . . . until we wound up making everything worse. Now there was nothing left but hurt. And hope. That was the thing that got you in the end. The hope.

"Think I'm gonna stew," I said.

"Course you are. What else would you do? So . . . and I know I'm gonna regret this . . . why did you call me down here?"

"I've got a new client."

"I'm thrilled for you."

"I don't know his name."

"Really?"

I took out my phone and pulled up the e-mail that had hired me. Rodriguez read it once, then read it again before sliding the phone back across the bar.

"I knew I shouldn't have come."

"Raymond Perry?"

"Told you it was interesting."

We'd taken our conversation to a booth. The TV was still on, but my cop friend had lost interest in himself.

"How long has it been since he skipped out?"

"Two years," I said.

"Feels more like ten. Last I heard they'd spotted him on an island somewhere."

"He's been 'seen' in the West Indies. Before that it was Paris, British Columbia, and Bangkok. All in the past year and a half."

"Our own little Whitey Bulger."

"More like a ghost."

"You ever meet him?"

"Once. At Kustok's wake."

Walter Kustok was a Chicago cop. He'd been on the job less than six months when he knocked on the front door of a South Side bungalow. An estranged husband fired three times through the closed door and killed Kustok where he stood.

"What did you think?" Rodriguez said.

"Ray came in by himself. No limo, no entourage, no speech. Just paid his respects to the family. Then he went to the bar and drank with Kustok's buddies until close."

"I heard about that."

"He was a politician, but I liked Ray. At least that night I did."

Rodriguez grunted and took a sip of his bourbon. "Who's dropping all the cash to find him?"

"Don't know."

"Did they deposit the first hundred?"

"It's sitting in an account with my name on it."

"You touched any of it?"

I shook my head.

"You gonna?"

"Why, you need a loan?"

The detective fed me a grin. "Depends on what you want me to do."

"I was thinking you could get someone in Financial Crimes to put a trace on the account."

"As it happens, I have someone down there who owes me a favor. Thing is, these people aren't likely to have left any tracks."

"I know, but I figure it's worth a shot."

Rodriguez shrugged, then sat up in his seat. "There we are. Hey, turn it up."

The bartender hit the volume, and we watched as Rodriguez stood behind his boss who was droning on about how the baby they'd found was healthy. No ID as of yet, but the Chicago PD was working on it.

"I look like a fat fuck," Rodriguez said.

"I heard TV does that to Latinos."

"You ever watch Telemundo? We were made for TV."

"The Irish were made for TV."

"The Irish were made for a coffin. It's called the sun, Kelly. Give it a try sometime."

The news package ended, and a tall brunette began talking about the investigation.

"I thought they interviewed you?" I said.

"Must not have made the final cut. What else is new? So, let's get back to all that money."

"Will you have your finance guy look at it?"

"Sure."

"He won't make any waves?"

"Nah. This guy's good. If they left any fingerprints, he'll find 'em."

"Thanks."

"That's it?"

"What do you know about Ray's wife?"

Rodriguez frowned. "Marie Perry? Not much. She's Billy Bones's daughter. High society, charity type. Ran around Springfield like a queen until they slapped the cuffs on Ray."

"And now?"

"Now? Expiration date's long gone."

"She's not that old."

"It's not the years, Kelly. It's the miles. I don't think she's even in town anymore."

"She's got an office two blocks from here."

"No kidding. Who cares? Better yet, why do you care?"

"Marie Perry was with the governor when he disappeared."

"Actually, she wasn't with him. That's the whole point. Listen, the wife is a pariah. When Ray skipped, he left her flat. No one wants to touch her. No one wants to be seen with her."

"How about her father?"

"Bones? Hell, he's deader than she is. Besides, from what I hear they hate each other."

"Why's that?"

"Don't know. Some family bullshit or something. Any way you look at it, Marie Perry's not in a position to be advancing you a hundred G's."

"I didn't say she hired me."

"Then what? She helped Ray disappear? Please. Since the day he skipped, her life's been fucked. And that's a fact."

"She thinks I'll never find him."

"She's right. So take the money, wherever it's from, and run."

"You remember Eddie Ward?"

"No."

"He was the electrician who took the elevator down twelve floors with Ray."

"How could I forget?"

"Eddie was in the federal building that morning to work on a Dippin' Dots machine. That's freeze-dried ice cream."

"I know what Dippin' Dots are."

"The machine was licensed to a corporation named Double D Entertainment. I looked up the registered agent. It's a guy named Paul Goggin." I wrote the names out on a napkin and pushed it across the table. Rodriguez wasn't impressed.

"So what?"

"Eddie's disappeared. I got a funny feeling Goggin might be right behind him."

"When you say 'disappeared,' what exactly do you mean?"

I glanced at the detective's glass. "Maybe I should get us another one before we get started?"

"I already opened up a tab. It's in your name."

CHAPTER 7

Rodriguez and I talked for another half hour. He promised to see if he could dig up anything on the whereabouts of Eddie Ward or Paul Goggin. Before he left, Rodriguez urged me again to empty the hundred grand out of the account before it disappeared of its own accord. I told him I'd think about it and followed him out the door five minutes later. I hailed a cab and looked out the window as we crawled through the evening rush on Lake Shore Drive. I had the cabbie get off at Fullerton Avenue and head west until we hit Lincoln. Then we backtracked a couple of blocks and pulled up in front of a bar with a hanging sign of a gigantic carrot.

Sterch's had been a tradition on Lincoln Avenue since the early seventies. The place was, and always had been, a drinkers' bar. Serious drinkers. The kind who put their keys and money on the bar because they knew they were gonna be there awhile. I walked in around half past five. The bar was full, and there wasn't a TV in the place. Boxing gloves and carrots hung from the ceiling and walls. An ALCOHOL FUTURES chalkboard was pegged above the register. On it were the names of six or seven regulars who'd had drinks bought for them in absentia or had been too lubricated at the time to take advantage of someone's largesse. Beside the board was a stack of citations from the city of Chicago for violations of its no-smoking laws and a white-and-black sign that read: THE MORE CORRUPT THE STATE, THE MORE NUMEROUS THE LAWS. TACITUS. In the back of the place, the bar had been kind enough to set up its own no-smoking section. It consisted of an empty rectangle made of aluminum tubing and hanging a foot or two from the ceiling. Nice.

I caught the bartender's eye and ordered a longneck Bud, then took my beer to a seat by the window and watched the people walk past. I'd been coming into Sterch's a couple of times a week for the past few months. The "craic," as my Irish-born friends liked to call bar conversation, was "mighty" . . . even if you were just listening. Which is mostly what I did. Listen to the chatter, drink my beer, and stare out the window. She usually caught the 5:45 bus up Lincoln Avenue. She used to drive to work, but now she took the bus. Sometimes, it ran a little late. Tonight was one of those times. Rachel Swenson was the second-to-last person to get off. She wore a black jacket with a collar she lifted against a sudden patter of rain. Rachel hustled across Lincoln and turned to urge someone behind her to beat the blinking light. She stretched out her hand and laughed. My eyes tracked back through the crowd, hunting for her companion. A couple of taxis cruised into the intersection and blocked my view. Then they laid on their horns just for fun. By the time the people and cars had cleared, Rachel was gone. As was her friend.

I had two more beers at Sterch's and eavesdropped on the conversations floating through the place. At a table to my left, a man and woman were comparing Royko to today's crop of scribblers. Not much of a comparison. Not much of a conversation. Behind me, a couple of guys debated the merits of our mayor. One guy thought he was setting himself up for a run at the White House. The other figured that to be a lateral move at best. And not a very smart one. My mind wandered back to Rachel, standing in a soft rain in the middle of the street, living her life and filling it up with people. I figured that was a good thing. No matter how much it hurt. I finished my beer, picked up my money, and headed out.

Maggie's nose was at the front door as soon as I cracked it. She ran around in circles until I opened up a cabinet for the dog food. Then she was all business, sitting at attention, eyes riveted on my every move. I filled her bowl, crouched down, and stared at her. She held my gaze for about ten seconds before her eyes flicked toward the bowl.

"Maggie."

Her eyes came back to mine and held on for another thirty seconds. Then the drift again, accompanied this time by a soft whine.

"Mags."

She barked once and slapped her tail against the floor. I nodded toward the bowl. She dove in up to her ears. Ten seconds later, she was done. I pulled her leash off a hook sunk into the wall.

"Park?"

She streaked to the front door and sat. I leashed her up, and we walked three blocks to a field next to a local middle school. The rain had stopped and the turf was just wet enough to be sloppy. Springer-spaniel weather. I unsnapped the leash and threw a tennis ball into the night. Mags brought it back and dropped it at my feet. I threw it again. The city felt empty—the only sound the metal clink of Mags's tags as she ran. I thought about Ray Perry. Maybe he was on a beach somewhere. Maybe he was dead. Maybe someone just wanted him dead. The tennis ball rolled against my shoe. I picked it up and looked at Mags, tongue out, tail thumping against the grass. I tossed the ball from hand to hand and smelled the smoke and sweat of Sterch's coming off my clothes. Mags barked. *I'm still here,* she said. I wound up and leaned into a throw. When I was in high school, I played center field. No one ever ran on me. If they did, it was at their peril. A couple of years back, I took a bag of balls out to my old position. In my mind and heart, I knew I could still do it. Then I picked up a ball and fired toward home plate. The mechanics were fine. Better, even, than I could have hoped for. The ball, however, barely reached the pitcher's mound. I remembered taking a look around. Maybe they'd changed the dimensions of the diamond. Maybe I was in deep center field. I grabbed another ball out of the bag and tried again. This one rolled up on the mound and bounced off the rubber. My shoulder was on fire down to my fingertips. I told myself I just needed to build up the arm again. If I came out once a week for a summer, I'd be back to where I was. That's what I told myself. Then I threw the bag of balls into the trunk of my car and slammed it shut.

I got back to the apartment around 8:00 p.m. No messages. No e-mails. I made myself some mac and cheese and threw in a can of tuna because I thought I needed the iron. I wasn't sure if tuna had any iron, but figured the mac and cheese didn't and the upgrade couldn't hurt. When I was done, Mags licked the bowl clean. Maybe she needed some iron, too. I fixed up a pot of coffee and took a cup into the living room, where I sat down with my laptop. Mags curled up on the other end of the couch and stared at me. I googled Ray Perry and began to pick through articles. Then I googled his wife. The picture I pulled up was taken at a community forum years ago. Even in the best of times, Marie Perry's face was better seen through the lens of a camera. Some people were just like that. Not unattractive in real life, just never quite living up to the magic of being "photogenic." I studied the elegant set of her chin and clean line of her jaw but couldn't find any of the pain I'd seen today. Still, there was something inescapably sad wrapped up in Marie Perry's smile, and I wondered where it came from.

I clicked the photo shut and opened up my black notebook. On the first blank page, I wrote down three names. EDDIE WARD. PAUL GOGGIN. RAY PERRY. I drew a line between WARD and GOGGIN and wrote VENDING MACHINE underneath it. Then I drew a line between PERRY and WARD and wrote ELEVATOR RIDE. Off to one side I scratched out MARIE PERRY and drew a final line between her and her husband. I stared at my little diagram for a while, then logged on to the website for the Illinois State Board of Elections. After about an hour, I had a working list of Ray Perry's major donors from 2005 through 2010. My routine was the same. I took each name in turn and did a search for any media coverage. Then I did a litigation search, cross-referencing the donor's name against civil and criminal court cases filed in Cook County. The donor list was an impressive one. A lot of high rollers. A lot of corporate money. I didn't really know what I was looking for but figured I'd recognize it when I saw it. It wasn't the best plan, but right now it was all I had.

I took a sip of coffee and typed in a name off the list. Hi-Top Construction. It was an Illinois corporation that had donated almost two million dollars to Perry spread out over three years. I pulled up the articles of incorporation for Hi-Top from the secretary of state's office. The company's registered agent was a local lawyer named Albert Striker. I shuffled through my handwritten notes. Striker had also acted as the registered agent for another Perry donor, an outfit called Eagle Cement. Neither company listed any corporate officers other than Striker. Not unusual, but interesting. I plugged Striker's name into the state's database. Five more corporations popped up. One of them, Railway Steel, was also on the Perry donor list.

I got up and poured myself some more coffee. Then I walked back into the living room and opened a fresh document on my laptop. Under the heading STRIKER GROUP, I typed the names of the three privately held corporations. Between them, they'd donated more than eight million dollars to Ray Perry over three years. When I expanded the window to five years, the donations jumped to more than fifteen million. Each outfit had won bids for significant highway construction projects during Perry's time in Springfield. I dug into the online clips and pulled up details on the state contracts. I printed out some articles and added names to my list. Spokesmen, contractors, more lawyers, a half-dozen vice presidents. Around 1:00 a.m., I found the entity I'd been looking for—Beacon Limited, a holding company that appeared to own all of the other outfits. Not surprisingly, Albert Striker was the only individual listed on Beacon's corporate charter. I put the name in caps and highlighted it in bold. By 2:00 a.m., I'd gone through two-thirds of the donors and filled up twenty pages with notes. I'd identified a couple of other key Perry supporters and listed them alongside the Striker group. I turned off the computer, collected my handwritten notes, and locked them away in a drawer. Then I drank a glass of whiskey and smoked a cigarette by an open window. Maggie was curled up on the floor of my bedroom and yawned when I came in. She gave me a quick scan to see if I had any food, then went back to sleep. I lay in bed and stared at the ceiling. Smart dog. Stupid owner.

CHAPTER 8

Spyder sat in the dark at a large round table, surrounded by an array of glowing computer screens. He accessed a display to his left and cycled through a series of cameras they'd set up in the apartment. Then he picked up a cell phone and punched in a number.

"I'm watching him sleep," Spyder said.

"Alone?"

"Unless you count the dog."

"So you got everything installed?"

"We've got every room covered. His landline and every keystroke on his laptop as long as he's in the apartment."

"How about his office?"

"No-go. The building's got some quirky things going on with its wireless reception, and he just installed a fairly sophisticated alarm system."

"Can you beat it?"

"Of course, but it might take some time."

A pause. "Let's just focus on the apartment for now."

"Fine."

"Why are you calling?"

"He spent a lot of time online tonight."

"Looking at what?"

"I'm sending it to you now. There's a lot, so it's gonna take a while to get through."

"You take notes like I told you?"

Spyder stared at the pad of paper by his elbow. "Filled up half a notebook."

"Give me the highlights."

"He pulled up stuff on Perry like you thought. Then he started digging around in the state database for donations to Perry's campaign and corporate records." Spyder edged the notebook a little closer. "Spent some time with a company called Hi-Top Construction. Another called Beacon Limited."

"Stop."

Spyder waited. He hated this cloak-and-dagger bullshit, but the pay was too good to pass up.

"Did he make any calls?"

"Nothing," Spyder said.

"You sure?"

"Hundred percent. We don't have coverage on his cell phone, but I would have heard the call."

Another pause. "Take a look out the window."

Spyder was sitting in the front room of a third-floor apartment. The room had three windows that looked out at Kelly's building across the street. Spyder had the windows covered. Now he reached out and tweaked one of the blinds.

"Can you see his place?"

"You know I can."

"We're gonna have someone follow this guy in the morning. I want you to coordinate with them."

"It'll be early. I'm guessing this prick doesn't like to sleep very much."

"We're not paying you to lie around in bed. Call me when he's up."

Spyder snapped his phone shut and considered a half-dozen ways he could cut his boss's throat. Unfortunately, the man didn't have a name or a face, so Spyder would have to content himself with the ten K wired into his account every other week. He turned up the audio levels in the apartment so the sounds would wake him when Kelly got up. Then Spyder zipped himself into his sleeping bag. He thought about the rifle in the closet. Another ten thousand. Per body, no less. Spyder smiled and closed his eyes. At the end of the day, it was all about the money . . . and pretty easy money at that. Spyder couldn't have been more wrong.

CHAPTER 9

I sat on an overpass, sipping coffee and staring down at the Eisenhower Expressway. It was just past 6:00 a.m., and a crew from Hi-Top Construction was arriving at the job site. There were ten of them in the pickup. Two up front in the cab. The rest piled into the back. A man with a belly like a cast-iron tub got out of the front and opened a gate so the truck could drive through. The work area ran for almost two miles and was bounded on both sides by a black privacy fence. The pickup stopped near a Hi-Top trailer, and the men in the back climbed out. I pulled a small set of binoculars from my jacket pocket for a better look. The men were dressed in dark pants and long-sleeved shirts. Each carried some sort of suitcase. One wore what looked like a priest's collar. Iron Belly gestured for them to put their luggage in the trailer. Then he began handing out picks and shovels. The workers hefted their tools and lined up at a long table on the far side of the trailer. That was when Iron Belly brought out the vodka.

I punched in a number on my phone. Jack O'Donnell picked up on the first ring.

"What do you want?"

"Hey, Jackie. I figured you'd be up. How you doing?"

"I thought I was doing fine. Now, I'm not so sure." For ten years, Jack O'Donnell had worked for the *Chicago Tribune* as their transportation editor. Now he ran an industry newsletter called *The Guard Rail.* O'Donnell had spent his professional career studying the men who broke rocks and built highways for a living. If there were bodies buried under the blacktop, O'Donnell knew how to find them. Whether he'd tell me was another matter entirely.

"Where are you?" O'Donnell said.

"I'm sitting on the Ike. Looking at a work site."

"Which job?"

"Just past Twenty-Fifth Avenue. Let me ask you a question. You ever hear of an outfit called Beacon Limited?"

"Fuck you, Kelly. Everyone knows Beacon."

"Not me. Not until last night."

"They like to spread their business out over a bunch of subsidiary contractors, but they're one of the biggest players in the country. What do you want with them?"

"You sound a little tight, Jack."

"I'm fine."

I looked again at the site. The workers were still clustered around the table. Iron Belly was passing out orange vests.

"You got some time, I'd like to pick your brain."

Silence.

"Jackie, you hear me?"

"I heard you. You want to talk about Beacon?"

"Just a couple of questions."

"It's never just a couple of questions. Not with you."

I waited.

"Let me think about it."

"You got my number?" I said.

"I got it. Make sure you pick up when I call."

"Fine, Jackie. I'll talk to you."

O'Donnell cut the line. I sat for another minute, watching the ebb and flow of early morning traffic, light stuff streaming smoothly around the construction zone. I started up my car and drove down onto the highway, parking just inside the fence and walking toward the work crew. As I approached, I heard a babble of voices. Best I could tell, all of it was in Polish. I got to within thirty feet before someone noticed me.

"Hey." It was the priest. He had a cold hot dog, no bun, in one fist. There were more dogs piled on the table along with two half-gallon jugs of vodka and a stack of paper cups. The priest said something to me I didn't understand, so I smiled. He smiled back. The other workers moved closer. Some had paper cups full of vodka. A couple had shovels. I nodded as they broke out again in Polish. Then Iron Belly stepped out of the trailer.

"Who the fuck are you?"

"Name's Kelly." I stuck out my hand. Iron Belly didn't take it.

"You're trespassing."

"Sorry. I'm an insurance investigator. Looking for a man named Albert Striker."

"Never heard of him."

"He works for a company called Beacon Limited."

"Never heard of it." Iron Belly glanced at his work crew, then back at me. "Now piss off before someone gets hurt."

"Can they understand a word of what we're saying?"

"They understand enough to kick your ass."

I nodded and smiled at the crew. "You just pick 'em up at O'Hare?"

Iron Belly grabbed a shovel. Up close, I could see the rotted holes where his teeth used to be and a wad of tobacco stuck in his cheek. "You want to play fuck-fuck, mister. I love to play fuck-fuck."

I wasn't sure whether his Polish army would stand and fight. Or just offer me a drink. Either way, I'd stirred the pot. And that was enough for one morning. I was halfway back to my car when I saw them. Four of them. Not Polish. Not illegal. One had a red beard and a bat in his hands. They spread out in a semicircle. Red Beard did the talking.

"This your car?"

"It is."

He swung the bat and spiderwebbed the passenger's side of my front windshield. "You're trespassing."

"You work for these guys?" I said and hooked a thumb back toward the trailer.

Red Beard nodded. He was six feet plus. Maybe two thirty. And the smallest of the bunch. "This is how we give out tickets to trespassers." He smashed in a side window. "Next time, it's your fingers. After that, knees and ankles. You understand what I'm saying?" He turned and started in on the passenger's-side door. That was when I pulled out my gun and shot him in the thigh. Red Beard went to the ground with a heavy grunt.

"Next one goes in the kneecap," I said as the other three circled. "Whoever catches it walks with a limp for the rest of his life."

I waited to see if anyone wanted to play hero. Hired help usually didn't, and this bunch was no different. They pulled Red Beard to his feet and began to back up. He cursed and tried to come at me again, but his leg buckled. I figured he was the leader and was glad I'd shot him first.

"Back away from the car," I said.

They gave me fifty feet. I insisted they give me fifty more. Then I slipped in the front seat and started up the car. I ran over a half-dozen cones as I pulled out of the work site and back onto the Ike. I was two miles down the road, windshield nicely smashed and no one in the rearview mirror, when my phone buzzed. It was Rodriguez.

"You up yet?"

"Up and out," I said.

"Where are you?"

"Just went for a run."

"Sounds like you're driving."

"What's going on, Vince?"

"I got a little information this morning on one of your pals. Paul Goggin."

"Where is he?"

Rodriguez gave me Goggin's last-known address. It was one all Chicagoans found their way to sooner or later: 2121 West Harrison Street. Also known as the Cook County Morgue.

CHAPTER 10

Rodriguez was waiting in a lobby paved in squares of green and white linoleum. He didn't say a word, just motioned for me to follow. We were buzzed into the morgue by a receptionist sealed up in her own Plexiglas tomb. Rodriguez led me down a dingy hallway to a small office with more linoleum, a table of gunmetal gray, and two folding chairs. Rodriguez pushed out a chair with his foot and slapped a folder on the table.

"What's this?" I said, taking a seat and flipping the file open.

"It's the paperwork on Goggin."

I pushed it aside. "Got a question for you. Beacon Limited."

"They own companies that build roads."

"Big outfit?"

"The biggest. Why?"

"Would you be surprised if their subsidiaries use illegals for some of their grunt work?"

"I'd be surprised if they didn't."

"So it's not something anyone should get too excited over?"

"Fuck, no. What's this about?"

"Nothing."

"What did you do?"

"You really want to know?"

"Probably not."

"Smart man." I opened up the folder again and pulled out Goggin's autopsy report. It was dated three and a half months ago. The cause of death was given as massive head trauma. Underneath that was a space for manner of death. Someone had typed in the word: HOMICIDE.

"The body's gone, I take it?"

Rodriguez eased his long frame into the other chair and tilted back against the wall. "Long gone."

"So why are we here?"

"You won't believe it."

"Try me."

"Four months ago, Goggin's driving down the Dan Ryan. Kid pushes a rock off an overpass and puts it right through his windshield."

"A rock, huh?"

"Goggin was killed immediately. We arrested the little prick a day later."

"Your case?"

"Nah. The detectives who handled it are good. They developed some information in the neighborhood, brought the kid in, and got a confession."

"Where is he now?"

"Sitting in county, waiting on a trial date."

I noticed an envelope clipped to the back of the file. It was thick with photographs.

"Mostly autopsy stuff," Rodriguez said. "There's a few shots from the scene."

I flipped through the photos. Massive head trauma was an understatement.

"The kid claims he's innocent?" I said.

"Aren't they all? He'll cut a deal."

I pulled out a photo of the car with the body removed. The windshield was gone, and the front third of the roof on the driver's side was crushed.

"Hell of a rock," I said.

Rodriguez leaned over for a look and grunted.

"Can I talk to the kid?" I said.

"What are you thinking?"

"Don't know. Where's the car?"

"Probably down at the pound."

"Let's go take a look," I said.

"At the car?"

"The kid, Vince. Let's go see the kid."

CHAPTER 11

The kid's name was Roderick Hampton. I read through his case file as Rodriguez drove us down to the jail. Hampton was sixteen years old. He lived two miles from the crime scene and had been arrested the day after Goggin's death. According to the file, Chicago detectives had developed a CI who stated that Hampton had bragged about hurling the rock off the bridge. Two locals subsequently came forward and claimed to have seen Hampton running off the bridge at or around the time of the crash. Hampton had been appointed a public defender and would be tried as an adult.

"This happened at three-thirty in the morning?" I said.

Rodriguez looked over. "So what?"

I went back to my reading. Rodriguez pulled into the lot at the jail, and we got out. Cook County Jail is the largest of its kind in the country. It covers ten city blocks and houses almost ten thousand inmates. Rodriguez led us through security to the prisoner-intake area. It looked like a terminal at

O'Hare, except all the passengers were murderers and rapists and all the flights were nonstop to hell. A row of cages ringed the outside of the room and were filled to capacity. Someone yelled Rodriguez's name, but he kept going. In the center, jail employees sat in front of green computer screens and processed detainees into the facility. We charted a diagonal path through the human debris. To our left, a heavily muscled Latino was sitting in a chair, helping a woman decipher a series of symbols and numbers carved on his chest. She took a picture of the tattoos and typed some information into her computer. The Latino looked up and rattled his cuffs.

"Rodriguez."

"Jimenez. What are you in for?"

Jimenez shrugged. Rodriguez glanced at the woman who talked as she typed. "Strong-arm robbery. Assault."

"Next time I see you, we go to that place. For the empanadas." Jimenez was still talking as we walked away.

"Buddy of yours?" I said.

"Come on." Rodriguez led me out of the intake area and down a long, dank corridor. A line of fifty men stood in their bare feet, hands on their heads, faces pressed against a wall made of gray cinder block. Opposite them, two correctional officers stood on an iron bench and yelled instructions. A third officer picked through a collection of shoes, sneakers, and boots that had been scattered down the hall.

"Let's hang for a minute," Rodriguez said. "Let 'em process these guys."

The officer picking through the shoes came up with a length of plastic sharpened to a wicked point. He laid it on the bench beside three other shanks, a set of brass knuckles, and a coil of thin wire wrapped around a pipe. Halfway down the line, a prisoner collapsed on the floor and started to spasm. One of the officers on the bench gave Rodriguez a look and motioned us past. We walked down the line, stepped around the man on the ground, and turned into a short hallway. Another officer stood in front of a door. He had a length of chain and a couple of sets of cuffs on a loop at his belt.

Rodriguez flashed his badge. "Roderick Hampton in there?"

The officer nodded. "You guys don't have any weapons?"

They'd taken our guns at the door. The officer patted me down anyway. Then the door opened, and we were inside.

"You got any cigarettes?" Hampton was cuffed and reached out with both hands.

"You know you can't smoke in here," Rodriguez said.

"Everyone smokes in here."

Rodriguez narrowed his eyes. "I know you, Hampton?"

The kid's lip was split and puffy. It cracked and bled when he smiled. "You arrested my brother, Marcell."

"Marcell Hampton. That's right. He was hooked up with Six Corners."

Hampton shrugged like that was news to him.

"How's it been?" I said.

"Put a beating on me first thing. But they do that to everyone."

"Your brother still inside?" Rodriguez said.

"He's doin' twenty at Stateville. I get over there and he'll take care of me." Hampton nodded his head like he was hanging on to that thought for all he was worth. I didn't blame him.

"You want your lawyer in here?" Rodriguez said.

Hampton looked around. "In where?"

We all laughed, and the kid relaxed a bit.

"Why'd you throw that rock off the bridge?" I said.

"Didn't do it."

"Then why are you here?"

Hampton turned his palms up in his lap. Then he opened

up a window in his head and climbed out. After that, Rodriguez and I were alone for a while.

"Roderick," I said.

He blinked and came back slowly. "Huh?"

"Can you stand up for me?"

The kid's cuffs jingled as he got up. He was five and a half feet. Maybe an inch more.

"How much do you weigh, Roderick?"

His eyes danced across to Rodriguez, then back to me. "Dunno."

"Okay. Sit down." I took out a fresh pack of cigarettes and pushed them across the table. My business card was tucked inside the wrapper. "If it gets really bad, tell your lawyer to give me a call." Then I left. I knew Rodriguez wasn't happy, but he followed me out anyway.

"What the hell was that?"

We were sitting in the front seat of the detective's car, staring at a run of perimeter fencing that sectioned off the jail's parking lot from the street.

"I wanted to see the kid."

"I told you he claimed he didn't do it."

"Hampton weighs what? Hundred thirty, hundred thirty-five pounds?"

"So what?"

I held up the investigative file. "You read this?"

"I looked through it."

I took out the picture of Goggin's car, roof crushed almost flat. "What do you suppose did that?"

"I don't know. A big rock."

I slapped a second picture on the dash. It was a shot of a flat slab of concrete, maybe three feet long. "That's what went through Goggin's windshield. Thing's gotta weigh a hundred pounds, easy."

"Let me guess," Rodriguez said. "You want to interview the rock?"

"It's a chunk of concrete. And I'd like to try and just pick it up." I took a third photo out of the file. "This is the overpass Hampton was supposed to be standing on. Notice the fence that runs the length of it. Gotta be at least six feet high."

"So what?"

I slid the photos back in the file and flipped it shut. "There's no way Hampton lifted that slab over that fence and heaved it onto the Dan Ryan. Not that kid. Not at a hundred thirty pounds."

"Maybe he had help."

"Your two witnesses say he was the only guy on the overpass."

"They're not mine. And maybe his accomplice ran the other way."

"You believe that? And why are two witnesses watching a highway overpass at three-thirty in the morning anyway?"

A county sheriff's bus rumbled past, hitting a pothole full of black water and splattering our windshield with specks of mud. Rodriguez flipped on his wipers, and we both watched them work.

"I got things to do today, Kelly."

"The kid was framed, Vince."

"Let me guess. You think it all ties into Ray Perry?"

"I'm not there yet."

"Have you tapped the retainer?"

"No."

"My finance guy did a quick trace on your money. It came in through a tangle of off-shore accounts. He thinks it's gonna be tough to track down the ultimate source."

"I'm not surprised."

"I asked him if the money still spent like cash. He said it did."

"What's your point?"

"Enjoy the dough and let Ray live on a beach somewhere. If the case on Hampton's bad, I'll make sure he gets sprung."

"Can't do it, Vince. You couldn't either."

Rodriguez flipped off the wipers and put his car in gear. "You headed downtown?"

"You gonna help me on this?"

Rodriguez sighed and pulled out of the police lot. Being the eternal optimist, I took that as an enthusiastic yes.

CHAPTER 12

I picked up my car at the morgue and headed north, stopping at The Bagel on Broadway. I got a sack of sesame seed bagels from the tiny Jewish lady hiding behind the counter and walked down to my office. I'd just schmeared one with cream cheese when my phone flashed with Jack O'Donnell's number.

"Just thinking of you," I said.

"What do you want to know about Beacon?"

I put down the bagel and pulled out my notes from the night before. "You ever hear of a lawyer named Albert Striker?"

"Doesn't ring a bell."

"That's funny."

"Why?"

"Beacon is made up of at least five subsidiary corporations and a half-dozen limited partnerships."

"I told you. That's how they do business. Spread the work around. Keep a low profile."

"So if I drive by a job on the road, I'm gonna see five different logos on five different trucks?"

"Right, but it all funnels back to Beacon."

"And who runs the show?"

"What do you mean?"

"Who's the boss?"

"Each outfit's got its own president, own engineers. All that crap."

"And Beacon?"

"Beacon never gets its hands dirty."

"So you don't know who runs Beacon?"

A pause. "What's your point?"

"Albert Striker."

"I told you. Never heard of him."

"Striker's listed as the registered agent for Beacon. He's also the incorporating officer for Beacon's subsidiaries."

"You said he was a lawyer."

"He's Beacon's sole legal representative in Illinois. At least as far as I can see."

"So go talk to the guy."

"The address listed in the corporate charter is now a taco stand."

"Call him."

"His phone number goes to a recording."

"Listen, I've been covering these guys for more than a decade. Beacon is just a shell. If you want information, you talk to one of the subsidiaries."

"If I want information on a job, sure. But I want to know who the principals are, who owns the whole thing. If you can't help me, Jack, that's fine." I picked up my bagel and started to chew.

"The job site you were at this morning . . ."

"What about it?"

"A man was shot."

"Son of a bitch."

"They took him to the hospital, but no police report was filed."

"Are you calling for a statement?"

"You don't want to fuck with these guys, Kelly. Even if you do carry a gun."

"I'm not looking to fuck with anybody. Someone takes a bat to my car, however, and we're gonna have a problem."

"Yeah, well . . ."

"Why did you call, Jack?"

"Give me an e-mail where I can get hold of you."

I gave it to him. "What's going on?"

"Right now, nothing. In a few days, maybe we should talk."

"Can you give me an idea of what we'll be talking about?"

"Not over the phone. I'll drop you a note."

There was a soft sound in the hallway. I looked up. Marie Perry stood in my doorway. "I'll wait to hear from you, Jack." I hung up. "Come on in."

She was wearing a black sweater, straight-leg jeans, and suede boots with low heels. Her hair was the color of winter wheat; her eyes looked like a couple of cold blue stones. "Is this it?" she said, taking in my workplace at a glance.

"It's better if you're wearing sunglasses. Or drunk. Then again, what isn't?"

She walked over to my bookcase and picked out a copy of *Oedipus Rex.* Then she put it back and pulled out Euripides's *Iphigenia at Aulis.*

"You know the story?" I said.

"A man cuts his daughter's throat to appease the gods and gain himself money, glory, and power."

"Very good. But Agamemnon was a king. And Iphigenia was saved."

"Agamemnon was a man. And he intended to kill his own child so his army would be allowed to sail to Troy." Marie slipped the book back into its slot on the shelf. "Do you work alone?"

"Just me and the ghosts. Why don't you sit down?" I nodded at an empty chair. She waved me off. I nudged the paper sack on my desk.

"Bagel Deli. Best thing this side of Manhattan."

She shook her head.

"Suit yourself." I finished my bagel and pretended not to notice when she finally sat. She put her bag, a big black leather one, on the corner of my desk and crossed one leg over the other. I wiped my hands with a napkin and smiled.

"I didn't expect to see you so soon, Ms. Perry."

"But you did expect me?"

"I'm not sure why, but yeah, I thought you might get in touch."

"How's the investigation going?"

"Haven't found Ray yet, if that's what you're after."

"Ray's dead, Mr. Kelly. Or as good as."

My chair creaked as I moved closer. "If this is a confession, I'm going to have to find a tape recorder."

The smile stretched across her face like a spiderweb spun from the finest silk. "I'm the last person who would want Ray dead."

"Did you love him?"

"And if I did . . ."

"You might be more likely to kill him."

"Have you ever been married, Mr. Kelly?"

"No."

"Why not?"

I didn't know the answer to that one. And didn't especially like to think about it. "I've been in relationships."

"A relationship isn't marriage. The latter has consequences, especially when you're married to the governor of Illinois."

"You mean it isn't all about Christmas at the mansion?"

She recrossed her legs and sighed. Maybe it was all just a

nuisance. Maybe it was the speech she'd intended all along. I couldn't tell but was happy to listen.

"Here's what happens," she said. "You fall in love with a person. Or rather the *idea* of a person. You ever done that?"

"I'm not sure."

"I'm not surprised. Then you get married and discover what you really have. It's never what you thought, but perhaps it's something you can live with. Usually not. So you get divorced, if that's your thing."

"And that wasn't your thing?"

"Not an option. Not for me and Ray. So we became partners."

"Partners in what?"

"Raymond Perry, Inc. Charity events, fund-raisers, one rubber-chicken dinner after another. You become best friends with people you barely know. And once you do know them, you wish you didn't."

"Sounds great. You want some coffee?"

She didn't say no, so I got up and began to fix a pot. She continued with the lecture.

"You're not in love anymore. If you ever were. You're too mature, too sophisticated, for anything so trivial. You're a team, a partnership, a walking, talking 'greater good.' Or so you tell yourself. Along the way, of course, you also stuff yourself with entitlement, arrogance, and an overwhelming sense of self-importance. Movies are especially wonderful."

"Movies?"

"Two people, together in the dark. You don't have to touch. You don't have to talk. And you don't feel guilty at the end of it because you did neither. Maybe you can even discuss the film later if it was a good one. Movies are a blessing.

"You take a lover if you want. Usually for the sex. But you're discreet. You don't embarrass the partnership, because that's not good business."

"And that's what marriage was for you?"

She looked at me with her pale bruises for eyes and didn't flinch. "I was a coward. Just like everyone else."

"What does that mean?"

"I liked being Ray's wife. I liked being first lady." She shrugged. "Maybe I liked the power, I don't know. But I hid myself from the rest of it. Sprayed a little perfume over the rotting corpse and opened a window. That was my marriage at the end, Mr. Kelly. And I miss it every day."

There was truth intertwined with the lies. Where one ended and another began, however, I had no idea. I wasn't entirely sure she did either. The coffee was ready, so I poured us both a cup.

"You ever hear of a company called Beacon Limited," I said.

A tinge of crimson swept into her cheeks, and her lips tightened into a thin line. "Of course, I have."

"Why's that?"

"They were one of my husband's biggest donors."

"Is that all?"

"Ray took care of that end of the business, Mr. Kelly. All I know is that they were generous."

"What about your father?"

"My father and I aren't close."

"Was he close to your husband?"

Her chuckle was spare and raised the flesh on the back of my neck.

"Something funny?" I said.

"My father's an opportunist and a predator. And he looks after one person. Himself. Ray realized that and kept him at a distance." She put her coffee down and glanced around my office. "I must say I love the picture you paint. Sophocles and Euripides on the bookshelf, a gun on your hip. Tell me, do you bed your clients as well? Or is that just in the movies?"

"Is that what you came here to ask me, Ms. Perry?"

"I came here to tell you to leave this alone. Nothing good will come of it."

"I'm supposed to see Karen Simone this afternoon."

She took a black leather wallet out of her black leather bag and slipped a silver dollar on my desk. "A dollar says you fuck her before you ever find Ray."

"You know me that well?"

"I've been bought and sold myself a few times. So, yeah, I think I do."

"Keep your money."

She palmed the dollar and put it back in her wallet. Then she put the wallet back in her bag. "It wouldn't be fair anyway."

"How's that?"

"I know Karen and you don't." She got up to leave. "Take care, Mr. Kelly. Let me know if you find out who you're working for."

"And if I find Ray?"

"You won't find Ray, Mr. Kelly. That much I'm sure of."

CHAPTER 13

A sloppy rain had begun to fall over the city. I hailed a cab on Broadway and made my way downtown. During his time in public life, Ray Perry had built a big part of his image on the back of a charity he and his wife had started called Chicago's Children in Crisis. The Perrys had run Three C together for the better part of a decade. Two years before Ray disappeared, Marie Perry walked away from the charity. Karen Simone took her place. And so the whispers began. I scrolled through a few of the articles on my phone as the cabbie maneuvered through traffic. It had started out innocently enough. A line in the *Trib* about the governor seen spooling pasta with an aide at a local restaurant. Then a second item about a power breakfast with a young woman at the Peninsula hotel. A free local rag called the *Observer* was the first to go for the red meat. Pictures of Ray and Karen Simone crossing the street together in Los Angeles. Back in Chicago enjoying lunch. Stepping off a private jet in Springfield. The idea of a possible affair had just started to percolate in the local press when the grand jury's indictments for Ray came down and eclipsed everything. I dug into the body of the *Observer* story but couldn't find any background on Simone. So I studied the grainy photos. The more I studied, the more I realized why Marie Perry had been willing to wager her silver dollar. The girl was small and lithe, with tangled blond hair, full, thick lips, and a well-scrubbed freshness that was the particular province of youth. She was the kind of girl men took risks for. It was etched all over Ray Perry's face as he helped her out of the back of a car. And if I could see it in a news photograph, I was pretty sure Marie Perry had felt it in the flesh.

My cabbie pulled up to the front of Northwestern's Prentice Women's Hospital and mumbled something I couldn't understand. I shoved some bills through the partition and got out. Prentice seemed closer to the Four Seasons than a hospital. Valet parkers in red coats scurried back and forth out front, picking up cars and dropping them off. Pregnant women and their male handlers pushed through revolving doors into a cavernous and carpeted lobby. To my left was a check-in area, to my right a flower shop, gift shop, Starbucks, and three separate lounges. All we needed was some booze and a decent bartender.

I checked my gun with security and took the escalator up one floor. Three C's "headquarters" consisted of a single suite tucked away at the back end of a corridor full of administrative offices. The reception area was empty, save for a black metal desk and pictures of poor kids looking down at me bravely from the walls. Three C had been a hot charity when Ray was in the mansion. At one point, they ran after-school art classes in Chicago's public schools, a mentoring program for teens as well as school-lunch programs, health screenings, and even sex-education counseling. When Ray was indicted, however, the money dried up, and the programs withered and died. Which led me to wonder what the hell Karen Simone did every day when she came to work. And who paid her.

I called out to see if anyone was home, then wandered behind the receptionist's desk and down a short hallway. There were two doors, both closed. The first opened into a small conference room. The second was locked. I walked back out front. Karen Simone was waiting.

"Mr. Kelly?"

"Sorry. Just poked my head in the back. Karen Simone?"

She was wearing dark blue jeans and a short-waisted black jacket over a silky, cream-colored top. Her lips were brushed in pale pink, and her hair was pulled back from her face. She moved like an athlete, light and confident. When she shook my hand, I could feel the strength in her grip. Her skin smelled like cut lemons.

"Why don't we talk in here?" She swiped a card through a reader and pushed open the door that had been locked. "Take a seat."

I found a hard-backed chair. Karen settled herself behind a desk sketched in sleek lines of brushed aluminum. Her smile was a force of nature—so easy and open it had to be fake. Her office, on the other hand, was a closed book. No photos, no diplomas. Not a clue as to who Karen Simone was, where she'd been, or where she was headed.

"You mentioned on the phone this was about Ray?" Karen sat up straight, hands clasped in front of her as she spoke.

"I'm investigating his disappearance."

She nodded and threw some more wood on the smile. The young woman wasn't going to offer up any information on her own. Fair enough. I'd come with questions.

"If you don't mind my saying," I said, "this place looks like a ghost town."

"I don't mind you saying."

"Is this the whole operation?"

"We did have three adjoining offices on this hall but had to let them go as the leases expired. Ray left us some money in a trust, but it's only going to last another six months or so. After that . . ."

"You say 'us,' but are you the only employee left?"

"We have a staff of volunteers who work here, at Prentice. That's always been our core. Critical-care infants."

"How about six months from now?"

"Unless we can find the funds, we shut down."

"And where do you go?"

She shrugged. "I don't know. Back east."

"That where you're from?"

"My parents are dead. I don't have any family to speak of. I was kicking around after school when Ray Perry gave me a break. A huge break, actually."

I nodded and we sat. Myself, Karen, and the gray elephant, tucked away in a corner, thumbing through a copy of *People.*

"Go ahead and ask about it, Mr. Kelly."

"Why don't you just tell me?"

"Fine. It ruined my life for a while. I'm sure it hurt the governor and his wife. I know it hurt them. But it ruined me. I was in a relationship at the time . . ."

"So there wasn't anything going on between you two?"

She raised her chin a fraction. "Between me and Ray? No, there was never anything going on."

"No attraction at all?"

"Have you ever met Ray?"

"Once."

"Everyone I knew was attracted to him. In that respect, I was no different. But it was more as a mentor . . ."

"And?"

"Pictures lie, Mr. Kelly."

The questions were hard, and I thought she might waver.

I guess I expected it. But she never came close. Karen Simone was nothing if not a study in poise.

"The police must have talked to you after Ray disappeared?" I said.

"The FBI. On several occasions. I know they followed me. And I think they might have even tapped my phone. Is that possible?"

"It's possible. So, what do you think?"

"About Ray?"

"Why did he skip out? How did he manage it?"

"I'll tell you what I told the investigators. I assume he disappeared because he didn't want to go to prison. But he never said a word about it."

"Okay."

"His wife hates me. She tries to hide it . . ."

"Actually, she doesn't try to hide it at all."

"Oh."

"Do you two have any sort of relationship?"

"We meet once a month to go over finances for the charity. She never says much."

"Marie thinks Ray might be dead."

"Why would he be dead?"

"I don't know. There were no signs of anything? Something small, maybe?"

"Ray and I had breakfast the day before his sentencing. He told me he was going to stay involved in the charity from prison. That he had some money put away for Three C. It would become his lifeline to the world. He was sad. Reflective. But about to vanish? No."

"Scared?"

"Of prison, sure. But that was it."

"You two must have talked at some point about the stories that came out? About you and him?"

"I told you. They hurt him. But maybe not as much as you think."

"Are you telling me there *were* other women?"

She shook her head. "Ray loved his wife. But the thing between them was broken. And he didn't know how to fix it."

We both paused. A moment of silence for the marriage of Ray and Marie Perry.

"You ever get that boyfriend back?" I said.

"It probably wasn't going anywhere anyway."

I stood up. "Thanks for the help, Ms. Simone."

"I'll walk you out."

We made our way down the hallway, past the empty spaces and frozen faces of smiling children.

"Does it get lonely in here?" I said.

"I keep busy. On the phone with our volunteers. The hospital. Bill collectors." She touched my shoulder as we reached the front door. "Can I ask you something?"

"Sure."

"Do you think you'll find him?"

"I don't know."

"Can you tell me who hired you?"

"That's two questions. I was hired through an intermediary."

"So you don't know who you're working for?"

"That's right. Why do you ask?"

"I don't know. Maybe answering one question might lead to solving the other."

"I don't necessarily want to put Ray in prison. In fact, I'm not sure what I want to do besides talk to the guy. If he should call . . ."

"I hope he's safe somewhere. And I hope he never calls."

"But if he does . . ." I took out a business card. She held it between her fingers.

"If Ray gets in touch and is all right with it, I'll call you."

"Thanks. I hope you get to keep the doors open here."

"You mean that?"

"Sure, why not."

"You ever been inside a NICU?"

I shook my head.

"Do you have kids?"

"Never married. No kids."

"You say it like you mean it."

"You want to show me the NICU, Ms. Simone?"

"You want to see it?"

"Probably be the best part of my day."

We took an elevator up to the tenth floor. Karen talked as we rode.

"Prentice's NICU is state-of the-art. It's where they keep all their critical-care infants. They also run the Safe Haven Program next door."

"That where they keep the abandoned kids?"

"Prentice is designated as an area where parents can safely and legally abandon their infant, no questions asked. If the child's healthy, Safe Haven places him or her with an adoption agency. The parents can remain anonymous and are given a bracelet with a number that identifies the child."

"And what if the parents decide they want their kid back?"

"They have sixty days to reclaim the child. After that, they waive all rights. Safe Haven has its own designated area, but it's technically attached to the NICU and is set up to take care of preemies and other critical-care infants in addition to any abandonment cases. This way."

We stepped off the elevator. Karen flashed her ID at a security guard and got me a temporary pass. We pushed through a set of doors and walked down a long corridor. I didn't see any nurses or doctors. No gurneys or machines with paddles. Not even a tongue depressor taped to the wall. Karen stopped at the end of the corridor and opened another set of double doors. On the other side were a sink and some liquid soap.

"We need to wash up before we get near the kids." Karen turned on the water and pushed up her sleeves. When she was finished scrubbing, I did the same.

"How many babies do they keep in here?" I said, reaching for a paper towel.

"This is one of several nurseries. They keep anywhere from six to eight infants in each one. This way." Karen pushed through a final set of doors and into the NICU. Here the place finally looked and sounded like a hospital. Machines beeped and buzzed. People scurried back and forth with stethoscopes and charts. To my left were a half-dozen open pods. Each held an infant. I looked at the first, sealed up in a glass incubator. His head was turned to one side, and he had a tube threaded up his nose. His chest was moving quickly, and he could pretty much fit in the palm of my hand.

"Preemie," Karen said over my shoulder.

A nurse came around the corner and stopped in her tracks when she saw me bent over the child. Then she realized I was with Karen and brushed past us.

"Our volunteers are in here every day," Karen said. "They work with the staff. Talk to parents. Babysit their other kids if the parents bring any with them."

We exited the NICU at the far end of the same hallway. To my left was a glassed-in viewing area. I stepped forward and took a peek. A room full of infants peeked back. In the front row, one stretched and blinked his eyes open.

"Hey, blue eyes," I said. The kid started crying. Karen cooed and tapped lightly on the glass. The kid settled almost at once.

"You've got the touch," I said.

"I've had practice. Listen, I need to run back inside and talk to the shift nurse for a moment. You want to wait?"

"Take your time."

I watched her walk away, waved good-bye to the kids, and wandered a little farther down the hall. Around the corner I found a door. The sign above it read SAFE HAVEN PROGRAM. I walked into a small outer office with a thick piece of glass running the length of the opposite wall. On the other side of the glass was a woman. She was white, middle-aged, with a large shelf for a forehead, small black eyes, and thick, colorless lips. Her name tag read: AMANDA MASON. REGISTERED NURSE.

"Can I help you?" Amanda's voice sounded more metallic than human. I chalked it up to the intercom and hoped for the best.

"I work with Detective Vince Rodriguez. We found the infant in Lincoln Park yesterday." I slipped my business card and ID under a slot in Amanda's window. She studied both carefully, then pushed them back.

"I just wanted to see the kid," I said. "Make sure he was all right." I pulled out a pen and scratched a number on the back of my card. "Here's the detective's cell if you want to check it out."

I didn't know if she'd call. I didn't know if Rodriguez would back me up. And I wasn't sure why I wanted to see the kid in the first place. But I did. So I gave her Rodriguez's phone number. Amanda looked at it, then reached under the desk and hit a button. A door clicked.

"Come on in."

On the other side of the glass was another nursery. Smaller than the NICU, this one had three pods arranged in a loose semicircle. Amanda met me just inside the door.

"This way." She led me to a pod with the curtain pulled back and pinned against the wall. At first all I saw were two legs kicking in the air. As I moved around the crib, I caught a flash of pink skin and a shock of thick, black hair. Then I stood over him. Smelling him. The kid made two tiny fists, stretched, and rounded his mouth into a perfect O.

"He just woke up," Amanda said.

"What's his name?"

"He doesn't have one."

"He should have a name."

"Is there anything in particular you needed?"

"No, I just came by to see how he was doing."

"He's a fine, healthy boy."

We both looked at the child again. He'd found our repartee boring and fallen back to sleep.

"How long will you keep him?" I said.

"A week, maybe two. They'll put him into one of the state facilities until they find a permanent home."

"How does that work?"

"There are a lot of couples who want infants, Mr. Kelly. The state will find him a spot."

"A spot, huh?"

I could feel Amanda Mason studying me. "You want to sit with him for a while?"

"I can't stay too long, but sure."

She pointed her heavy jaw toward an empty chair. "If he starts to fuss, let me know."

I thought I detected a hint of a smile as she walked off. And then I was alone. The kid opened his eyes and wrinkled his face in another bout of yawning.

"You look like an old man when you wake up," I said. The kid didn't offer much in the way of a response, so I watched his heartbeat on a screen. Tiny white waves surfing across a sea of dark blue. One of the machines buzzed once and stopped. I expected Amanda Mason to come running with her hair on fire, but nothing happened. Except the kid gurgled.

"I'm gonna call you Vince," I said. "You like that?"

He rubbed his toothless gums together and kicked his

legs some more. I took that as a yes. So I found a marker and scratched out VINCE on a Post-it Note. Then I stuck it above the crib.

"The real Vince is a hell of a guy," I said. "Besides, you kind of owe him."

The kid reached out with both hands, and I found myself bending forward, as if on a string, watching as he squeezed one of my fingers for all he was worth. I pulled back lightly, and his eyes widened.

"You got a good grip."

He squeezed again. I smiled. He smiled back, and I wondered why anyone would willingly give up even a moment with their child. Never mind stick him in the trunk of a car and walk away.

I gently tugged my fingers free and stood up. Along one wall of the pod was a row of photos. My gaze came to rest on the second to last. Marie Perry was seated, leaning forward slightly and warming her face against the bundle in her arms.

"Those are our volunteers . . ."

I almost jumped. Amanda Mason stood just behind me.

"Sorry, did I scare you?"

I smiled. "Must be those nurse's shoes."

"Do you know Ms. Perry?"

"Just what's in the papers."

"Yes, well, don't believe everything you read."

"No?"

"She's a wonderful woman. Comes in three or four times a week to hold the babies. Stays sometimes for hours."

"No kidding."

"Absolutely. I know what they wrote about her, but I just wish people could see everything."

I nodded back toward the crib. "Thanks for letting me get a peek at Vince."

"Vince?"

I pointed to my Post-it. Amanda's laugh was surprisingly soft. Almost youthful. "You named him?"

"That's the name of the detective who found him. You may want to pass it along to the agency."

"I will, Mr. Kelly. And we'll do our best to find Vince a good home."

I said good-bye to the kid and walked past the empty cribs. Then I was in the outer office again, looking back through the glass. Amanda Mason was testing the temperature of a baby bottle by shaking a few drops of formula on the inside of her wrist. She glanced up and caught me staring at her. The nurse nodded and didn't seem the least bit surprised. Then she bent over and slipped the bottle into the baby's mouth.

Karen Simone was just coming out of the NICU as I walked back down the hall.

"Sorry," she said. "Took longer than I thought."

"That's all right. I had a look around."

"Oh, yeah?"

"A pal of mine is a Chicago cop. He found an infant in Lincoln Park yesterday."

"I heard about that."

We started to walk toward a bank of elevators.

"They're keeping the baby here," I said. "I stuck my head in to see how he was doing."

"And?"

"He's healthy. He's happy. He's lucky."

"That was very nice of you to stop by."

A comfortable silence carried us the rest of the way to the elevators.

"Where are you headed?" I said and pushed the DOWN button.

"I was going to grab some lunch. You hungry?"

"I can't. How about a rain check?"

"Lunch?"

"I was thinking more like a drink."

Karen cocked her head. "Business or pleasure?"

"Probably an annoying combination of both."

A crooked smile touched her lips. "Next week might be better."

"Should I take that as a yes?"

An elevator arrived and the door opened. Karen got on first and held the door for me. "As long as it's nothing fancy."

"Are you saying you want to go to a dive?"

"I want to go somewhere that's not gonna freak out if someone lights up a cigarette."

"I know just the place," I said and hit the button for the lobby. Marie Perry and the image of a tumbling silver dollar flashed through my head as the elevator doors closed and the car began to drop.

CHAPTER 14

My lunch date was in Old Town, two miles and at least five decades removed from Karen Simone. Billy "Bones" McIntyre worked out of an office above Chicago's Second City Theatre. I pushed in off Wells Street and groped my way up a dark, twisting staircase. As I climbed, I could hear the patter of garbage cans in the alley and the thump of traffic in the street below. The stairs dead-ended in a landing with a single door made of pitted wood and pebbled glass. The letters on the glass spelled out DEMOCRATIC COMMITTEEMAN, except one *A* and a couple of *M*'s were missing. I turned the doorknob and walked in. Bones was sitting on a stage at the far end of a dusty hall. He had a cigar in full boil and was blowing clouds of blue smoke toward a tin ceiling. Bones was on the phone but waved me over. As I got closer, I realized the receiver had a cord that connected to a large black base unit. Then I realized the base unit had a rotary dial. Bones finished up his call just as I arrived.

"If you've got a subpoena, just leave it at the door." Bones seemed to like his little joke and sucked hard on the cigar. I watched his cheeks pump like tiny gray bellows and wondered when was the last time anyone in the Chicago media had gotten a picture of this guy.

"How you doing, Bones?"

"Like you give a fuck. Sit down."

Bones still had the voice of a politician—rippling like a cold river over hard stones. His appearance, however, hadn't fared nearly as well. In the twenty-five years he'd run Cook County, McIntyre had made a habit of wrapping himself in suits made of English wool, ties of Italian silk, and French cuffs all around. Today, he wore a threadbare pair of Dickies work pants, a blue sweatshirt with a hole under the arm, mismatched socks of green and gray, and a battered pair of Nike running shoes.

"What's with the phone?" I said.

"What do you mean?"

"It's got a rotary dial."

"So what? They tried to give me one of those push buttons. I told them to keep it."

Behind Bones was a large-than-life poster for the 1968 Democratic Convention. On the other side of the stage, Bobby Kennedy reached out of a convertible to tousle a small boy's head. From the phone to the politics, everything in the place reeked of throwback. Nothing more so than Bones himself. The man had once been a king maker, a guy who could get out the vote or kill it, depending on which way the wind was blowing off Lake Michigan. Bones had taken his retirement when the *Chicago Tribune* discovered he kept two women on the county payroll for the exclusive purpose of providing Bones with sex. The women were twenty-five and twenty-three, respectively. Bones was sixty-eight at the time. And happily married for fifty years.

"How's the wife?" I said.

"Faith? Never better, never better." Bones took a pull on his cigar and sent another stream of smoke spiraling toward a fan beating overhead.

"I'm here about Ray," I said.

Bones nodded. I could have said Daffy Duck, and Bones would have nodded like that was what he expected.

"You've been to see Marie." Bones didn't ask. He knew. And when Bones knew something, he didn't waste time with competing points of view.

"I talked to her, yeah."

He licked some old-man crust off his lips and laid the cigar, still smoking, in a cut-glass ashtray. Fifteen years ago, Bones had gone to a doctor who told him he had all five major risks for heart disease, plus a couple more the doctor had never heard of. Bones told the doctor he'd rather die than give up his cigars. The doctor told him that was a distinct possibility. Bones left the office that day looking to strike a deal with himself. According to legend, he never ate another piece of red meat, stopped using butter, and refused to drink any whole-milk products. He started running five miles every morning and hadn't missed a day in more than a decade. Gray sweats, Bears cap pulled low over his eyes, black socks instead of gloves wrapped over his hands, Bones became a lakefront fixture. And he always ran alone. That was Bones. Cigars and all.

"Why do you care about Ray?" he said.

"Someone hired me."

"Someone hired you. So you just jump in and start screwing with people's lives?"

"Your daughter seemed fine with it."

"Leave her alone."

"Where's her husband?"

"How would I know?" Bones flapped a hand around the empty hall. "You think I'm at the top of the food chain here?"

"Why did Ray disappear?"

"Thirty years in prison might do it for me. How about you?" Bones flashed the shark's-teeth grin of a Chicago pol.

"What do you know about a company called Beacon Limited?" I said.

The grin disappeared, and something even more unpleasant replaced it. "I did some work for them."

"What kind of work?"

"Consultant. But that was a long time ago. They were just a small outfit back then."

"And now?"

"Now, they're not so small. Let me ask you something. You been going around town asking about Beacon?"

"Every chance I get."

"You should smarten up."

"Do you know Albert Striker?"

"Beacon's attorney. Or at least he used to be."

"I'd like to talk to him."

"Might be tough. Albert died three years ago."

"Someone must have replaced him?"

Bones's cigar had gone cold. He took his time relighting it. "You don't understand Beacon, Kelly. It's not a company as much as an idea."

"So I've heard."

"Day-to-day business is handled through the subsidiaries. And they know nothing about the parent company."

"Someone must make the big decisions?"

"Dig if you want. All you'll find are more corporate layers. More dead ends."

"Was Ray involved with Beacon?"

"You know the answer to that. They were heavy contributors to the campaign."

"How about your daughter?"

Bones pulled the cigar from his mouth and let a little smoke leak out behind it. "Let's go get lunch."

He led me back down the stairs and across North Avenue. Bones waved a hand at the Old Town Ale House as we passed by. "Still do most of my drinking in there, but we're gonna eat at another place."

We stopped in front of a wooden building with a Hamm's poster in the window. The place looked abandoned, but Bones pulled at the door and it opened. Inside a young woman with sharp features and small, dull eyes slouched behind the bar. She wore jeans and a Bears T-shirt she'd tied off to expose her pale stomach. The woman was talking to a drowsy-looking guy with three days' worth of beard and an open Budweiser in front of him. The way she leaned over to talk told me they were sleeping together. But that was probably just me. Too many nights on a barstool at Sterch's. The guy hopped up when he saw Bones and hurried over.

"Mr. McIntyre."

"Bones. I told you, Bones."

"Bones. Great to see you. We were just opening."

I looked around. A couple of pitchers of stale beer were fermenting on the bar, and the floor was still sticky from last night. Most of the chairs were turned upside down on the tables, and the place smelled faintly of vomit.

"I thought I told you I wanted these women wearing clothes," Bones said.

The guy with the growth scratched at it. "I'll talk to her."

"Tell her to cover up that goddamn belly. What's your name again?"

"Darryl. Darryl Jones."

"How old are you, Darryl?"

"Thirty-two."

"Thirty-two. You like that stuff?"

"What stuff, Mr. McIntyre?"

"Forget it. Where can we sit?"

Darryl showed us to a booth and wiped it down with a dirty sponge.

"Couple of beers, Darryl." Bones looked at me. "Old Style, okay?"

I nodded. What the hell.

"An Old Style and an O'Doul's. And give us some soup. You like soup, Kelly?"

"Sure."

"Couple of bowls of that chicken soup I had yesterday. And some bread."

Darryl scurried back behind the bar. The girl showed up a minute later with two longnecks. She had her eyes down and midriff covered.

"Thanks, honey. This is for you." Bones pushed a twenty into her hand, took a long gargle from the O'Doul's, and thumped it down on the table.

"You got an interest in this place?" I said.

Bones hooded his eyes and winked. "Six months ago they were going to shut the place down. Guy asked me for some help. I paid off what he owed the county in taxes and took over the license."

"What do you know about bars?"

"What did I know about politics? We'll be fine." Bones jerked a thumb behind him. "Just poured a new patio out back. Gonna be a beer garden for the summer. City's bitching about the licenses."

"Let me guess, you're gonna take care of that?"

"I still got a little pull. Neighborhood pull, but what the hell. It's what I know. It's fun."

Darryl showed up with two bowls and a basket of bread. Bones was right. The soup was good—hunks of chicken, rich broth, and lots of rice.

"My daughter," Bones said and ripped off a crust of bread. His hands were thick and strong. In the barroom light they reminded me of my father, who beat his children sometimes because he liked the sound.

"What about her?" I said.

"We're not close."

"I've heard that."

"We did the thing for the press when Ray was governor. Family pictures. Magazine articles. All that happy horseshit. The truth is we haven't been close in years."

"Before Ray?"

"The problems go back earlier than Ray, yes. But they got worse once she was married." Bones used the crust to soak up some soup. It was hot and made the old man's eyes water.

"Did you and Ray get along?" I said.

"I liked him. I wasn't part of the inner circle, but we'd talk politics from time to time."

"Did you want to be part of the inner circle?"

"In 2006, Ray Perry went from never having held public office to governor of Illinois. And did it without breaking a sweat. It was like an old baseball skipper looking down his bench and finding the next Mickey Mantle at the end of it. You bet your ass I wanted to be part of it."

"But you weren't?"

"On the political side, no. But Ray was always good to me. Too smart not to be. And we never talked about Marie. Smart there, too."

"You think your daughter helped him disappear?"

Bones shook his head. "She wouldn't put herself out like that."

"Did she love him?"

"Marie isn't capable of love. At least not how you and I understand it."

I put down my spoon and leaned in, resting my forearms on the table. "You got something else to tell me, Bones?"

He gestured to my bowl. "The soup."

"It's not that good."

Bones stopped eating and hunched forward so his head hung between his shoulders. "Things happened after my daughter got married. Things the public never saw."

"The corruption charges? The trial?"

"This was personal."

An image of Karen Simone flashed before my eyes. "Another woman?"

Bones waved the notion away. "Marie might not have cared about Ray, but he loved my daughter. Almost as much as he loved himself."

"So what was it?"

"Once Marie got married, she went off the tracks. I mean she was always troubled, even as a kid, but this was different. Withdrawal, paranoia, deep bouts of depression. From what I understand, Ray had her on a heavy dose of meds and considered institutionalizing her."

"How about now?"

"No idea. She seems stable. At least from a distance."

"When was the last time you spoke with her?"

"A word hasn't passed between us since Ray skipped. I called. Left messages. Nothing."

"What do you want from me?"

"Did Marie hire you?"

"Confidential, Bones."

"Doesn't matter. I want you to let this whole thing go. Ray's not coming back, and we all need to move on. Especially my daughter."

"Maybe she doesn't want to move on?"

"So you help her. Make up something. Tell her whatever she needs to hear. Just put Ray Perry to rest. That's what I want. Nothing more. Nothing less."

"And why would I help you?"

"It's Chicago, Kelly. That's what we do." Bones ripped off another hunk of bread and dipped it in his soup. I got up to go, then stopped halfway.

"What if I told you your daughter already agrees with you?"

"In what way?"

"She's convinced Ray's never coming back. Believes he might be dead."

The old man shoveled the bread into his mouth and creased his face into a skeleton smile. "Then I'd tell you she's lying. When all else fails, she's always been pretty good at that."

CHAPTER 15

For the next week the case sat. Like a fisherman who'd cast his lines, I had to be patient, content to drift with the current and see if anyone bit. Every morning, I'd get up at 6:00 a.m. and go for a run. I'd usually start at the totem pole on the lake and work my way south, slipping past Belmont Avenue and Fullerton, along Oak Street Beach to Navy Pier. I'd watch the waves as I ran, gray walls of water rolling in from the east and spending themselves at the stone feet of the city. I'd think about the case, about the people and what went on behind their eyes. Back at my flat, I'd grab a quick shower, make some coffee, and be in my office by nine, poking through Ray Perry's past, following up on all the alleged "sightings," looking for a rabbit hole the former governor might have disappeared down. Twice during the week, I'd taken a detour from my routine. An unexpected detour but, somehow, maybe not. It was only a five-minute drive downtown and a short elevator ride up—to the Safe Haven Program at Prentice, and the kid I'd named Vince.

I didn't do anything spectacular on my visits. I'd show Vince the stuffed animal I'd brought—the first time a Chicago Bear, the second a Cub—and stick it up on a shelf next to his crib. Amanda Mason was always around. She claimed Vince knew who I was. I told her the kid smiled when anyone came up to the crib. She said yes, but he kicked his legs in the air when I showed up. And that was special. I thought Amanda was full of it, but I liked the idea anyway. So we sat by the crib and stared at the kid, smiling vacantly the way real parents do. Amanda would leave after a while, and I'd sit there alone and watch him. He'd watch me back. And kick his legs. And I felt special. Even if it was all make-believe.

It was during my third visit that I saw Marie Perry. I'd been there for an hour or so and was getting ready to leave when I caught a glimpse of her. She was in the reception area, talking animatedly to Amanda. The conversation seemed one-sided, Marie gripping the nurse's shoulder and bending forward until there seemed to be no space between the two. Suddenly, she lifted her head as if she'd caught a scent and turned, pinning me with a look through the thick glass. She walked into the nursery, Amanda trailing in her wake.

"Michael Kelly."

"I didn't realize you two knew each other," Amanda said, the confusion of my earlier lie tangled up in her voice. "Mr. Kelly has been coming in to sit with one of our abandoned infants."

"Have you, Mr. Kelly?"

"A friend of mine found a boy stashed in the trunk of a car. I come in to check on him."

"He's been in three times in the last week," Amanda said protectively.

"Where's the boy?" Marie said.

I walked her over to Vince's pod. Marie picked him up and cradled him. The kid's eyes danced, and he reached out to touch her cheek. For just a moment, I thought I saw the former governor's wife soften.

"He's beautiful." She turned to me as if he were mine.

"Yeah, he's pretty great."

"Do you have children, Mr. Kelly?"

"Just a dog."

"Would you like to hold him?"

I shook my head. "I just sit and watch. Talk to him sometimes."

Marie kissed Vince on the nose and laid him back in the crib. "He's beautiful."

She'd already said that, but I noticed that people tended to repeat themselves when they were around babies. I was no exception.

"Are you here to volunteer, Ms. Perry?"

"Not today. I just came in to talk to Amanda for a moment." She held out her hand. "It was nice to see you again."

"You, too."

"I must say, you surprise me a little bit."

"How so?"

"I don't know. I guess I didn't expect to see you hanging around a nursery."

"We all have our secrets, Ms. Perry."

Her hand slipped out of mine, and the cool, thin mask dropped back over her face. "Good-bye, Mr. Kelly."

"Actually, I'm heading out myself."

We walked back to the reception area together. Marie had a few more things to discuss with Amanda, so I rode the elevator down alone. Five minutes later, I was sitting in my car with a perfect view of Prentice's main entrance. Marie Perry came out and waited while one of the valets fetched her car. Then she got in and drove. I gave her a little room and followed. I wasn't sure why, but figured I had nothing to lose.

CHAPTER 16

The Women's Health Clinic on Chicago's North Side is as nondescript as a building can be. Jammed in between a currency exchange and a taco stand, the clinic has an exterior made of flat yellow brick, with no windows and only a blue sign by the door indicating the services provided inside. Marie Perry pulled up in front of the clinic at just after 11:00 a.m. She ignored a small knot of protesters across the street and walked straight into the facility. I parked at a McDonald's, got a coffee, and took a seat by a window that offered a good view of the action.

The folks out front weren't interested in Marie. She was a little too old to be a target. The next woman who arrived, however, was a different matter. She got off the number 50 bus at Armitage and Damen and walked across the intersection toward the clinic. The woman was in her early twenties, wearing jeans and a light blue hoodie pulled up over her head. Three people detached themselves from the group and met her almost directly in front of the Mickey D's. The one doing the talking was a middle-aged man, slight with ginger hair and a gentle, unlined face. He was wearing a tan jacket with a priest's collar poking out underneath. On either side of him stood two women. One appeared to be in her forties and wore a long-sleeved white shirt with CHOOSE LIFE spelled out in black letters across the front. The other looked like someone's grandmother. She carried a stack of documents in her arms and had a set of rosary beads wrapped between knotted fingers. The group moved slowly down the block, the young woman in the center, the activists orbiting, the procession looking like some strange sort of interconnected solar system. At one point, the woman made a move to cross over to the clinic, but the pull of the group was too strong. Gradually they shuffled her toward the entrance of the McDonald's. Then they were inside, taking a booth maybe fifteen feet from where I sat. The priest held the dominant position, directly across from the woman. The others spread out on either side. The priest kept his voice low, eyes fixed on his target.

"Here are copies of just a fraction of the medical malpractice suits filed against the clinic." The priest was feeding documents across the table. The young woman poked her head out from under the hoodie and gave the paperwork a sniff.

"We're concerned about your safety, Elena, as much as your child's," the priest continued. "There's another clinic less than two miles from here. It's a pregnancy and wellness center. Clean. Professional. Caring. They'll give you all the information you need. More important, you, and your baby, will be safe." The priest ducked his head, desperate to make eye contact. To no avail. He touched the arm of one of his helpers. "Marian can give you a ride over. She'll wait while you see a doctor, then give you a lift back."

Elena looked up. "Don't I need an appointment?"

The three smiled as one. "We can get you in this morning," the priest said. "No waiting." He began to nudge his way out of the booth. I got up and walked over.

"What's the rush, Father?"

The priest's mouth puffed open a touch; his eyes blinked rapidly. "Can I help you?"

"I'm not sure." I grabbed a chair, turned it around backward, and sat in it. "Our friend here has got a decision to make. And she should have the chance to make it herself, don't you think?"

I could feel Elena's gaze flicking back and forth, watching me, watching the priest.

"Absolutely," the priest said. "And the best decision, the right decision, is one that's well informed."

"Agreed." I picked up a copy of one of the lawsuits. "I see you gave her some information on the clinic across the street."

"It's a dangerous, dirty place," the grandmother said, then put a hand over her mouth and flushed.

I nodded. "Best though if Elena makes the call. What do you think, Elena?"

All eyes turned to the young woman. And the child she carried in her womb. Elena slipped off the hoodie and straightened up in the booth. She was Hispanic and younger than I'd thought. No more than fifteen or sixteen. For what it was worth, she was also breathtakingly beautiful.

"Maybe you could just leave me the address of the wellness center?" Elena flashed a row of perfect white teeth at the protesters. "I could give them a call and stop by."

"This is about the health of you and your child," the priest said gently. "Do you really want to wait?"

"I want to think about things. If that's all right?"

The priest covered the young woman's hands with his. He knew when a fish had spit the hook and didn't waste his time trying to recast. "Of course, of course. Thanks for your time, Elena . . ."

"Ramirez."

"Ramirez. Please call us if you have questions." With a silent glance at me, the priest slipped a card into Elena's hand

and left. His two helpers followed him out the door and across the street.

"How you doing?" I said.

Now that we were alone, Elena had retreated back into her shell. "I'm fine."

"My name's Kelly."

"Funny name for a guy."

"First name's Michael. Did you like what those folks had to say?"

She shrugged and studied the priest's card.

"It's called the Chicago Method," I said.

"What?"

"The approach they were using to keep you from having an abortion. It's called the Chicago Method."

"They have methods?"

"Everyone's got methods, Elena." I noticed a spark had returned to her eyes and kept talking. "The Chicago Method was developed by the Pro-Life Action League back in the eighties. It's a low-key, low-pressure approach. Notice they didn't show you any pictures of babies or even mention the word 'abortion.' The idea is to give you some information on the malpractice lawsuits and the health dangers of the clinic itself. Then offer an alternative."

"The wellness center?"

"Yes. And the wellness center might be a great place. But it also doesn't perform abortions. They leave that part out."

"So they were lying to me?"

I shook my head. "Not really. They were just giving you some facts. And skipping over some others. My guess is they're not bad people. They also can't make the choice for you. But I think you probably already knew that."

"How do *you* know so much?"

"You mean whose side am I on? I guess I like the underdog. That'd be you."

"I'm eight weeks along."

"How are you feeling?"

"I don't want to show. That's why I wear all of this." She held up her hands, stuffed once again inside the front pockets of the hoodie.

"You concerned someone's gonna find out?"

"I've just got to decide."

"Have you been to the clinic before?"

"I stopped by last week. Today was going to be my second visit. I guess I'm getting closer."

"What are you afraid of, Elena?"

"I'm not afraid of anything."

"Now who's lying?"

Her eyes were brown, flawed with flecks of green. Her thick hair shone, even under the flat, fast-food light.

"Are you afraid of the father?" I said.

She shook her head.

"Your family?"

She pulled out a wadded-up piece of paper and pushed it across the table. I unfolded the paper carefully. It was a police report dated four years ago. I started to read. Elena cut to the chase.

"My oldest sister, Lourdes, got pregnant when she was my age. My father took out a gun in our kitchen and stuck it under her chin. My mother watched from the doorway. I watched behind my mother. Just before he pulled the trigger, he moved the gun an inch so it blew a hole in the ceiling. My sister collapsed . . ."

Elena's voice skipped a beat. I waited.

"My father stood over Lourdes with the gun. He put it to her head and told her she was a *puta*. Told her she should pray it's not her brains on the ceiling. Lourdes began to say her Hail Marys, but she was crying and shaking and couldn't get them right. I remember she looked at me, and I felt ashamed so I left. The police came later." Elena nodded at the paper in my hands. "When I woke up the next morning, my sister was gone. I haven't seen her since. And I swore I'd never get myself that way. Not like Lourdes." She wrapped her arms around her midsection. "Yet here I am."

"What's your father's name?" I said.

"Rafael. Rafael Ramirez."

"Where did he get the gun?"

"He's a cop."

I skimmed the report. The investigating officer had concluded there was insufficient evidence to arrest anyone and characterized the shooting as an "accidental discharge of a weapon."

"Can I keep this?" I said, holding up the report.

"If I can get it back."

I took out my card and gave it to her. "How long until you have to make a decision?"

"Another month. After that, it gets dangerous."

"Think about what you want to do. What *you* want to do. Not a priest with lawsuits or old ladies with signs. Not some guy like me. Not your old man with a gun. *You* think about it and *you* decide. 'Cuz no one has to live with it but you. Okay?"

She nodded.

"Good. Call me when you know what you want, and I'll try to make sure it happens. Meanwhile, if it's all right with you, I might have a talk with your father."

"I told you he's a cop."

"I know how to talk to cops. I used to be one. How many brothers and sisters do you have?"

"Three sisters, including Lourdes."

"My e-mail's on the card. Send me her social security number, and I'll see if I can track her down. Cool?"

The card disappeared into one of her pockets, and Elena smiled. Impossibly beautiful. Impossibly young. Impossibly old.

CHAPTER 17

The rest of the morning was slow. The protesters spoke to at least three more women on the street, one of whom chose not to enter the clinic and was driven away by a member of the group, presumably to a date with the wellness center. Just before noon, the activists piled into a couple of cars and left. After that it got really boring. I ate lunch at the McDonald's, then kept myself busy by drinking coffee and trying to remember the entire roster for all six Bulls championship teams. I was halfway through ring number four when Marie Perry finally walked out of the clinic. By the time she hit the light at Armitage and Damen, I was three car lengths behind her.

Marie took a left on Damen and drove north until Diversey where she took a right. Four blocks later she took another left on Southport and pulled her black Lexus to the curb in front of Saint Alphonsus Church. The stone face of the church soared over the West Lakeview neighborhood, its copper-tipped steeple rippling and shimmering in the afternoon sun. I watched

Marie walk up the curved white steps and disappear inside. Then I followed.

The interior of the church was dark, and the air felt cool on my skin. Marie had taken a seat about halfway down one of the side naves. I waited a few minutes, then walked down the aisle and slid in next to her. She didn't seem surprised in the least to see me.

"You come here a lot, Ms. Perry?"

"Once a week for confession. Other times just to be alone."

"Sorry if I ruined that."

"Me, too."

I stared at the naked altar and thought about my own dusty history with Catholicism. I tried to remember the last time I'd been to confession, but couldn't.

"What time does it start?" I said.

"What's that, Mr. Kelly?"

"Confession?"

"In about an hour or so."

"Can I ask you a question?"

"You can ask whatever you want."

"Why does a woman visit an abortion clinic and then come to church directly after to pray and take confession?"

"Why does a man sit with an infant he doesn't know and will never get to see grow up? A man with no children himself and precious little chance of ever having any?"

"Touché, Ms. Perry, but I'd still like an answer."

"How does any of it tie into the job you're being paid to do?"

"Don't know yet. Probably doesn't at all."

"So you're just curious."

"I guess so."

She got up and left. I followed her down the aisle. We hit the back door and stepped into the sunshine. An old woman was coming up the steps. I opened the door and watched her go inside. Then we were alone again. Marie slipped on a pair of dark sunglasses.

"Could you answer my question?" I said.

Her head turned so I could read my face in her lenses. "Why do I attend church and work as a counselor at an abortion clinic?"

"That's what you do?"

"Yes, I counsel young women. I hold their hand and talk to them about their options, the procedure. And I'm there for them when it's over. Is that so hard to understand?"

"It just surprises me."

"Why's that?"

"I guess I think there's more to the story."

"A simple act of compassion isn't enough?"

"Things are rarely simple, Ms. Perry. You know that as well as anyone. So tell me the rest or not, but don't pretend it doesn't exist."

A pigeon burst out of one of the stone carvings cut into the face of the church and flew low over our heads before sailing across Southport Avenue. Marie took off her sunglasses so I could see her eyes while she spoke.

"When I was seventeen, I got pregnant. I was terrified of my father and decided to have an abortion on my own. The clinic wasn't properly licensed, and the procedure left me bleeding, half dead, and sterile. You were wondering what went on between myself and Ray? That's what went on. I didn't tell him until after we were married, and he never trusted me again." She kicked at the stone steps of the church. "There's your pound of flesh, Mr. Kelly. Bought and paid for."

She put her glasses back on and walked down the steps to her car. I watched her go, then went inside and sat in the dark and holy space. I thought about compassion. And human suffering. And marveled at how Marie Perry had become such an expert in each.

CHAPTER 18

Karen Simone called at a little after six that same evening. She wanted to cash in her rain check for our drink. After the day I'd had, I thought that was a fine idea. We met at Sterch's at eight. The bar was filling up and a cloud of blue velvet enveloped us as we pushed through the door.

"You forget how great that smells," Karen said.

"You don't strike me as a smoker."

She held up a finger. "Technically, I'm not."

"Let me guess. You want to soak up some secondhand smoke?"

"Is that against the law? Never mind, don't answer that. Why don't you find somewhere to sit and I'll get the drinks. What do you want?"

"Beer."

"Beer it is."

Karen headed toward the bar. I watched her bump her way through the crowd like a veteran, then turned to find us some seats. All the tables were taken, as were most of the stools they'd scattered around the place. A booth opened up to my left and I grabbed it. My usual perch at the window was also empty, but the booth seemed like a better choice tonight. I'd just settled in when there was some jostling and a knot of people dissolved. My throat went dry and a sudden heaviness filled my chest. The thick blond hair, slight build, and infectious laugh. All I could think of was Rachel. Then Karen Simone looked up, a beer in one hand and half of another spilled down the front of her jacket. A couple of men on either side were taking turns apologizing.

"Don't worry about it," she said.

One of them offered to stand her another round. She held out the half-empty pint to me. "That's okay. He gets this one anyway."

The two didn't recognize me, but I knew them as regulars. They hung around, talking to us for a bit, stealing a glance at Karen every chance they got. Finally, they drifted away and we were alone.

"Sorry about that," I said, pointing at the jacket.

"That's what dry cleaners are for. Cheers."

We touched our pints together. Karen took a look around. "I like this place. It's got that lived-in feel."

"That's one way to put it."

"What's with the carrots?" she said, pointing to a large fuzzy one hanging from the ceiling directly overhead.

"The owner used to dress up in a rabbit suit at street fairs and sell carrots for a quarter apiece. People loved it."

"Okay."

"It's Chicago. You know. Drinkers."

"I saw the sign behind the bar. Tacitus. That's great."

"The cops come in and write them up once a month for the smoking. The manager says the publicity he gets is well worth the fines."

"He's got me sold." Karen took a sip of her pint and licked a line of foam off her upper lip. "How was your day?"

"Long."

"Anything you want to talk about?"

"Probably not."

"You sure?"

"It's Marie Perry."

Karen raised her hands in protest. "Sorry I asked."

"That bad between you two?"

"Things are a little frosty, but I can handle it. So, what did she do?"

"Nothing, really." I squinted as a man at a nearby table blew a stream of smoke over our heads. "Ray ever mention any psychological problems?"

"With Marie? Not that I can recall. Why?"

"Just loose talk. You get a lot of that in this line of work."

"She's a hard woman, Michael. But crazy?" Karen shook her head. "I can't see it."

"Me neither."

We drank our beers and listened to the bar chatter around us.

"Can I ask you something?" Karen said.

"Is it about the case?"

"It's about your gun. I noticed you carry one."

"Mostly for show."

"But you've used it? I mean actually fired it?"

"I have."

"Does that bother you?"

"Shooting at another human being should bother anyone. If it doesn't, you've got a serious problem."

"Yet you choose to do it for a living?"

"I chose to be a cop. Then a private investigator. Like I said, the gun's a very small part of it. Why all the questions?"

"It's interesting. You're interesting."

"Not really."

"I find that people who think they're not interesting invariably are."

"And people who *do* find themselves interesting . . ."

Karen rolled her eyes. "We all know some of them."

My phone buzzed with an e-mail. It was Jack O'Donnell, suggesting a time and place for our meeting. I shook my head and slipped the phone back in my pocket.

"What is it?" Karen said.

"A friend wants me to meet him in the middle of nowhere tomorrow night."

"Who is he?"

"Just a guy. Used to work as the transportation writer for the *Trib.* Now he runs an industry newsletter on highway construction."

"Does it have anything to do with Ray?"

"Could be."

"Highway construction? I don't see the connection."

"Neither do I, but that's how things usually work." I pulled my pint an inch closer. "A case is like a ball of string. You pick one thread at random and start pulling. Eventually, it leads you to whatever's in the middle. At least that's the hope."

"So you really don't know where you're going?"

"I start out by asking questions, watch how people react, and decide what to do from there."

"You must piss off a lot of people?"

I grinned. "We're back to the gun again."

"Do you think you'll find Ray?"

"Maybe not, but I'll find something."

"You seem so sure of yourself."

"I'm Irish. We can't help ourselves."

"Touché." Karen tipped her glass my way, then paused.

"What is it now?"

"You're gonna say it's the beer talking, but I think I can help you."

"With Ray?"

"Yes."

"You're right. It's the beer talking."

"I've got good instincts about people. I could be your sounding board."

"And why would I need a sounding board?"

"Why not? I know Ray. I know a lot of his friends. In a few months, my charity will be shutting its doors, and I'll be on a bus out of town. Probably never to return."

"People have helped me before."

"And?"

"And some of them wound up dead."

That brought the conversation to a standstill . . . at least for a moment. "I don't plan on winding up dead, Michael."

"Neither did they."

"It's not like I'm going out on a raid or anything."

"You mean it's just talk in a bar?"

"That's it. Talk in a bar."

"Can't do it, Karen. Sorry."

"Why not?"

"I told you. Too dangerous."

"I already know you got a text from some highway guy. Tell me more about that."

I scratched my jaw. Karen sat patiently and watched.

"I'll give you one more piece of information. Just because you might be in a position to help. There's a company called Beacon Limited. You ever heard of them?"

She shook her head.

"They donated a lot of money to Ray and got a huge chunk of work out of it."

"What kind of work?"

"It's a little complicated, but they own a lot of other companies that build roads. Illinois roads."

"So what about them?"

"If you ever hear anything, just let me know."

"What would I hear?"

"I don't know. Probably nothing."

"You think this Beacon had something to do with Ray's disappearance?"

"It's possible."

Karen frowned. "It's not."

"Why do you say that?"

"Ray disappeared because he wanted to. Not because anyone forced him to. And certainly not because of some evil cabal of road contractors."

"So Ray was just trying to avoid the prison time?"

"Probably."

"You don't seem totally convinced."

"I told you Ray's personal life wasn't right."

"And when you say 'personal life,' you mean his marriage?"

"Bingo. You want another beer?"

I put a hand on her arm. "In a minute. So you're saying Ray disappeared to get away from Marie?"

"I think Ray loved his wife, almost to a fault. In some ways, his marriage was a life sentence. And that was probably just as hard as anything the judge was handing out. When he disappeared, Ray killed two birds with one stone. Whether he meant it that way or not, I don't know. But that's what happened. Now, do you want another beer or what?"

CHAPTER 19

We had two more beers, bummed a couple of cigarettes from the table next to us, and left around ten-thirty. I was hungry. Karen was starved. So we got in her car and drove. Actually, I drove. She sat in the passenger's seat and played with the radio. I tried three different places, two Italian and one Thai, but they were all closing up for the night. The last, a place in Ravenswood called Baffeto's, was still doing takeout. Baffeto's had a woodburning oven, and their thin-crust pies took only three minutes to cook. Sold. We got a large *margherita* pie and brought it back to my place. It was past eleven by the time we walked through the door. Maggie was waiting.

"She's adorable." Karen crouched to scratch Mags behind the ears. The pup liked that so much she rolled over on her back for the full treatment. I went into the kitchen to get us some plates and a couple of beers. By the time I got back, Mags was on high alert, wagging her tail and looking expectantly from me to the heavenly aromas emanating from the pizza box.

"Just ignore her," I said.

"Did she get dinner?"

"You have a dog?"

Karen shook her head.

"You can feed them dinner five times over, and they'll still be looking for number six. You mind if we take her for a quick walk?"

Mags was less interested in the walk than we were. After all, there was pizza in the house. We ate in the living room. The pie was great, thin and light with hunks of fresh mozzarella and a touch of basil.

"I thought Chicago only did deep dish," Karen said, reaching for another piece.

"Good?"

"Awesome." She folded up her slice and took a bite. "As you can tell, I was starving."

"Dig in. Otherwise, it goes to the beast."

Mags licked her chops once and moved a little closer to us and the pie.

"She's so cute."

"You should get one."

"I'd love to. Maybe once I settle down somewhere."

"So you don't think it'll be Chicago?"

"I don't have anything lined up. And there are cheaper places to live."

"A lot of not-for-profits in town."

"Yeah but . . ." Karen wiped her mouth with a napkin and took a sip from her beer.

"But what?"

"The community's a small one. And Marie Perry's name still carries a lot of weight."

"You think she's blackballing you?"

"I didn't say that. In fact, she doesn't have to. The publicity about Ray and me did that for her."

"Did you ever confront any of the media about the articles?"

"Confront how?"

"I don't know. Sue."

"To be honest, Ray caught most of the heat. And it all went away once the indictments came down."

"But you think it ruined your career in Chicago?"

"Maybe not. Maybe I just want to move on. It's not like I'm from here or anything."

"Where are you from?"

Karen picked a melted piece of cheese off her plate. "Okay?" I nodded. She gave it to Mags, who licked Karen's fingers clean. "I grew up all over."

"You said back east?"

"All over back east. My parents were killed in a car crash when I was seven."

"I'm sorry, Karen."

She held up a hand. "Thanks, but it was a long time ago. Anyway, at that age you're a tough sell in the adoption market. Couples came by to kick the tires, but no-go. I bounced around in foster homes until I was old enough to get out on my own."

"You put yourself through school?"

"Community college for two years. Then I wrangled a scholarship. So, you see? No roots. No ties. No need to stay in Chicago. How about you?"

"I was born here."

"How about the rest?"

"The rest of what?"

She looked around the apartment. "This? You? Your life? Gotta be more than late nights and guns."

"After Mags, it's all downhill."

"Come on."

"What?"

"Why isn't there someone in your life?"

"How do you know there isn't?"

"Is there?"

I carried the plates back into the kitchen. Karen followed.

"Not fair, Kelly."

I opened the refrigerator. "You want another beer?"

She shook her head. I popped one open and leaned against the counter. Karen parked herself on a stool and waited.

"You know the bar we were in tonight?" I said.

"Sterch's?"

"Yeah, Sterch's."

"What about it?"

"The truth is for the last couple of months I've been in there a couple of times a week. I sit in the window and wait for a certain bus to arrive from downtown. My ex is on it. She doesn't want to talk to me. I don't want to see her. But there I am. Twice a week, give or take. Getting my fix."

"Now, I'm the one that's sorry."

"Don't be. It's just a thing. A rut I'm in, I guess." I stared at the clock on my kitchen wall and wondered what time it was in hell.

"Can I ask you something else?" she said.

"More humiliation? By all means."

"Do you believe me? What I told you about me and Ray?"

"That there was nothing going on?"

She nodded.

"I believe you."

"Why?"

"I don't know. Instinct."

"You use that a lot in your job?"

"Have to."

"How's it working?"

I waggled my hand back and forth. "Fifty-fifty, but I'm still breathing. You want to go back out?"

I put on some music, and we settled on the couch. Karen

scooted close, and I put my arm around her. The music was Elvis Costello. Mellow Elvis. I listened to him sing about a girl named Alison and thought about one named Rachel. Then I thought about the one beside me. I could feel the rise and fall as her breathing slowed. When the music was finished, I got up carefully. Karen mumbled something and curled up on my couch. I got some blankets out of the closet and slipped a pillow under her head. Then I turned off the lights. I called to Mags, but she was laid out on the floor and not moving. I made my way back to my room and crawled into bed. The night was mostly quiet. I listened to the traffic below and the wind in the trees until I fell asleep.

Across the street, Spyder leaned back in his chair and rubbed his eyes. Then he picked up his cell and punched in a number.

"What?"

"You told me to call when he went to bed."

"Is he asleep?"

Spyder checked the monitor. "He's gone."

"Did he fuck the girl?"

"No. She's asleep on the couch."

"Can you see her?"

"I can see every room in the house."

"Why didn't he fuck her?"

"I don't know. He just didn't."

"What did he talk about?"

"He talked about Marie Perry."

"What else?"

"He's got an old girlfriend."

"We know about her."

"And?"

"It's being taken care of. You just keep listening."

CHAPTER 20

I woke to a buzzing in my ear. Maggie jumped out of bed and growled low in her throat.

"It's just my phone." I pulled the mobile off my nightstand. The message symbol was flashing. I clicked on it.

Why haven't you accessed your money?

Mags jumped back up on the bed beside me. I scratched her behind the ears and read the words again. Then I typed in a reply.

You mean the 100k?

The response was immediate.

Are you making progress?

I typed.

Hard to say.

My fingers paused over the touch screen. Then I typed some more.

Who is this?

I waited but got no response so I typed a final line.

I think Ray's dead.

Five minutes slipped by, but my client, if that's who it had been, was gone. Maggie jumped off the bed and stretched into a perfect downward dog. It was then that I remembered we had an overnight guest.

"Is she still out there, pup?"

Mags took that as a cue for breakfast and bolted out of the room. I threw on some jeans and followed. Sunlight poured through my living room windows. The couch was empty, pillow and blankets neatly folded and stacked on the floor. I could smell coffee and found a fresh pot brewing in the kitchen. There was a note beside it.

Michael,

Thanks for the bed. Not to mention the pizza and beer. Had fun last night. Love to do it again.

Your new sounding board,
K.

I fed Mags, poured myself a cup of coffee, and took the note into the living room. I liked looking at her cursive and wondered what the hell that meant. And why she hadn't stayed for breakfast. I was rereading the texts I'd received when my front doorbell rang.

"She came back for breakfast."

Mags wagged her tail. I walked to the front door and hit the buzzer. Thirty seconds later, there was a footfall on the stairs. I swung the door open. Andrew Wallace stood there with two cups in his hands. "I brought coffee."

"You don't seem too happy to see me," Wallace said.

"It's fine. How did you know where I lived?"

"It was on your business card."

"Oh, yeah."

We were in my kitchen. Wallace was sitting on a stool, his backpack on the counter beside him. "I e-mailed you last night. Told you I might stop by."

"Must have missed it. What time is it?"

"Almost eight. You want me to come back?"

"I just need to wake up. What's going on?"

"I pulled together some photos from the courthouse." Wallace zipped open his pack and slid out an iPad.

"From the day Ray disappeared?"

"Yes. There are only a handful of shots worth looking at. The first few are Ray and his wife together, waiting for the elevator to take them to the basement. Then I took three of Ms. Perry alone, waiting in the parking garage."

Wallace powered up the tablet. I yawned and took a sip from one of the coffees he'd brought. Awful. I found my own brew and watched over the grad student's shoulder as he began to open applications. "Did either of them say anything to you while you were taking the photos?"

"Ray knew I was there but ignored me. Which was fine. I don't think Ms. Perry ever registered me."

"Even in the basement?"

Wallace shook his head. "I don't think so. Not until the

end anyway. She just had this glazed look on her face. Here we go."

Wallace pulled up the first shot. It showed Marie and Ray standing in an empty hallway. Ray was looking away from the camera. Marie was staring at Ray. Wallace was right. She was locked into a thousand-yard death stare. Wallace clicked through a selection of similar shots from the twenty-fifth floor. Then we switched to the garage.

"The lighting wasn't very good here, so the pictures are grainy. This is Marie waiting for Ray's elevator."

The photo was clouded and taken from almost directly behind Marie. She had her hands jammed into her pockets and her head tilted up, watching a row of floor numbers strung out in pinpoints of light above her.

"These next two are from when the elevator door actually opened."

Wallace had angled to one side so he was just off Marie's shoulder. She was leaning forward slightly and peering directly into an empty elevator car. The light from inside the car was yellow and warmed one side of her face.

"This is when the door first opened?" I said.

"Yes. Here's the other shot I got. Maybe ten seconds later. She turned and looked straight at me."

The picture wasn't much help. The light from the elevator car was almost directly behind Marie, casting her in silhouette.

"Did she say anything?" I said.

"No. She just looked at me like I wasn't there. Then she pulled out her cell phone and walked away."

"Did you go over to the elevator?"

"I didn't even think about the elevator."

"Why?"

"I don't know. Why would I?"

"So what did you do?"

"I followed Ms. Perry. Tried to hear what she was saying

on the phone. I was thinking maybe her husband had gotten sick. Or decided to take another route out of the building."

"But?"

"When she got off the phone, I saw her face and knew it was bad. Like maybe Ray was dead."

"Did you take any more pictures?"

Wallace shook his head. "Didn't seem right. I mean I'm not really a journalist or anything. Anyway, ten minutes after that the cops arrived and all hell broke loose."

I pulled up the three parking garage photos and put them side by side on the screen. "You were standing right behind her?"

"For the first shot. I wanted to get Ray coming out of the elevator for the second, so I moved a little."

I got out my laptop and clicked on the photos I'd taken of the parking garage elevator. We studied the two sets of images.

"See anything?" I said.

"My photos have Marie Perry in them. Yours don't."

"Anything else?"

"The elevator door isn't open in any of your photos, so there's hardly any light."

I freshened my coffee and sat down again at the counter.

"What do you think?" Wallace said.

"I think you captured the moment when Marie Perry realizes her husband has gone missing."

"And?"

"And that's gotta be worth something." I enlarged the picture of Marie staring into the empty elevator car until it filled the screen. "Can you sharpen this up at all?"

"I tried to clean it up before I came over. I can zoom in a bit if you want?"

"No, leave it as is." I studied the profile of Marie's face. "Should she be more surprised?"

"I told you. She seemed sort of freaked out the whole time I was with her. Even up on twenty-five."

"Do you think she knew Ray was going to skip?"

"At the time I didn't."

"And now?"

"I still don't."

I went back to studying the picture.

"What are you looking for?" Wallace said.

"I don't know. Something we missed. Something that isn't there that should be."

"Like what?"

"If I knew that . . ." I paused, then glanced again at Wallace. "You still have access to the garage in the federal building?"

"Sure."

"Can you get us in today?"

"It's Saturday."

"Can you get us in?"

"Maybe. Why?"

I stood up and threw the grad student his coat. "Let's go."

It took us three hours to go over everything. First, we studied Wallace's photographs some more, then we walked through it all in the dim and dust of the federal building's parking garage. Then we took some pictures. By the time we'd finished, I was convinced. I didn't know if I could prove it, but I was convinced. And that was good enough. I downloaded Wallace's photos to my laptop. The grad student knew where Marie Perry lived and wanted to tag along, but I told him that wasn't going to work. The less other people knew, the better. So I went by myself and parked just down the street from her building—a three-story brownstone on Astor Street in the Gold Coast. She pulled up in a cab at about a quarter after six. It was raining lightly, and she held a newspaper over her head as she ran into the building. I gave her five minutes, then walked to the front door and pressed the buzzer. Her voice sounded tinny over the intercom.

"It's me," I said. "Kelly."

Silence.

"How can I help you, Mr. Kelly?"

"I found Ray."

More silence. Longer this time. I thumbed the grip on my gun. Then her voice came down again.

"First floor."

The buzzer went off, and I pushed inside. The lobby was mahogany and marble. A small table with fresh flowers stood by three mailboxes. On the other side was an old, graceful staircase. I started to climb. She met me at the landing and led me into her apartment without a word. I took a chair beside a cold fireplace and looked out at the drizzle. Across the street was a modest little shack known as the cardinal's mansion.

"You want something?" She held up a rocks glass with some amber-colored liquid in it.

"Whatever you got."

What she had was scotch. Not the cheap stuff either.

"I'm sorry about the church," I said. "You're right. It was none of my business."

Marie took a seat in the chair across from me. A side table stood sentry between us. "Am I supposed to say something?"

"There's a girl I met named Elena Ramirez. She tried to come into your clinic the other day."

Marie raised her eyebrows. " 'Tried'?"

"The protesters out front shooed her off, but she's been in before to check things out. And she'll be back."

"I'm not sure what you want from me."

"Elena's sixteen years old, eight weeks pregnant, and scared out of her head." I took out a folded-up sheet of paper and put it on the table. "That's a copy of a police report that was filed four years ago when Elena's older sister got pregnant. The old man's still got his gun, and Elena thinks he'll use it for real on her."

"So she wants to have an abortion?"

"She doesn't know what she wants. And she needs someone to help her figure it out."

Marie skimmed the report, folded it up, and tucked it by her side. "I've never met Elena, but I'm sure I can track her down. As for Mr. Ramirez . . ."

"You worry about the girl. I'll take care of the old man."

"Fair enough." Marie took a sip from her scotch and set the glass down on a wooden coaster. She blinked her frozen eyes once and waited.

"Your father thinks you're crazy."

"I told you. My father's a predator. And you'd be well advised to stay clear of him."

"I know how to find Ray," I said.

"You know *how* to find him?"

"I know how he got out of the courthouse. And I know who helped him."

"Why are you telling me?"

"I thought you'd want to know."

"I didn't hire you, Mr. Kelly."

"You need to know."

"Fine. I'm listening."

I pulled up my bag and took out my laptop. "There's a grad student I met. Getting his master's in architecture. He's been hanging around the federal building on and off since college."

"Doing what?"

"Taking pictures. He was there the day Ray was sentenced. Up on the twenty-fifth floor with both of you. Then again in the parking garage. Maybe you remember him?"

"What does he look like?"

"Thirties. Light brown hair. Pretty fit."

"I vaguely remember a man who came down after me in the elevator. But I'm quite sure I was alone when Ray's elevator arrived."

"You weren't. The grad student took these photos." I turned around the laptop and clicked on a picture. "You're waiting for your husband in this first one."

She studied the picture, the muscles in her jaw working overtime.

"Here's the one I want you to focus on," I said and pulled up the second picture. "This is the moment when the elevator door opens and you realize Ray's not in the car."

She gave the image a long look and sniffed. "I remember it. So what?"

"Look at the photo."

"I did."

I opened up another file and clicked on another image. "This is a picture I took an hour ago. The same open elevator door, shot at roughly the same angle. I had the grad student stand in for you."

"You're lucky you're not working for me, Mr. Kelly. I have a feeling you wouldn't last long."

"You don't see it?"

"See what?"

"In the picture I took today the back wall inside the elevator car is bathed in light. The entire wall. It comes from a single fixture mounted in the car's ceiling."

"Fascinating."

"Now look at the picture of the empty car you're staring into." I pointed. "There's a shadow across a portion of the back wall. Why do you think that is?"

She glanced again, first at one photo, then the other. "No idea."

"It couldn't have been cast by you because you were still standing outside the car."

"All right, it couldn't have been cast by me."

"There was someone in that elevator car, Ms. Perry. Someone tucked away in the corner so only you could see him—but big enough to cast a shadow."

"One of us *is* insane, Mr. Kelly. Fortunately, it's not me."

"The grad student told me you were the only one who actually looked into the elevator. Then the door closed, and you called upstairs to sound the alarm."

"So?"

"What happened to the elevator car itself?"

"Why don't you tell me?"

I closed up my laptop. "Whoever was in that car took it to an upper floor. I haven't got the records yet, so I don't know exactly where. Then he got out and disappeared into the crowd."

"Ray couldn't have done that. They had the building locked down almost immediately and weren't letting anyone leave. Besides, they have cameras on every floor. Someone would have seen him."

I smiled. "Not if Ray was already gone."

"I'm not following you."

"You're following me, Ms. Perry. Hell, you're a mile ahead and stepping on the gas. Eddie Ward was the guy in that car when it hit the parking garage level. He was part of the plan from the start. When Eddie got on the elevator that afternoon he was carrying a canvas tool bag. In the bag were work clothes identical to his own. I think Ray stepped onto the elevator at twenty-five and changed into those clothes. He slouched Eddie's Cubs hat over his head, put his own clothes into the bag and got off on the thirteenth floor dressed as Eddie. Then Ray took the stairs to the ground floor and walked out of the building before the alarm was ever raised. Eddie rode the elevator to the basement and was crouched in the corner when you peeked in. While everyone ran around looking for Ray, Eddie took the car up one or two floors and got out. He hung around the building, showed the cops his ID, and eventually gave a statement to police."

"Truly unhinged."

"Maybe. But if I'm right, it will all be on the security

tapes. And easy to find once you know what you're looking for. Eddie arriving with the bag in the morning. Ray dressed as Eddie getting off on the thirteenth floor with the bag in his hand. And then the interesting part. A second 'Eddie' getting off somewhere else in the building. Without a bag. No one's ever looked for that. But it won't be hard to spot. And then it all comes back to you."

Somewhere outside, a crack of thunder boomed and echoed. Marie Perry started to say something, then paused and took another sip of her drink. When she smiled, it gave me a quick chill.

"What do you want?"

"Tell me if I'm right."

She chuckled and shook her head. "Do your best. See if I care."

"This can go one of two ways, Ms. Perry. I can go to the feds and let them run you down. Or I can feed you in pieces to the press. Either way it's not gonna be fun."

"And what if you're wrong?"

"I'm not. And even if I am, it won't matter. Everyone will believe it just because they want to. You'll be fresh meat all over again, and people love that."

The apartment had gone quiet again, save for a clock ticking away on the fireplace mantel and the steady fall of rain outside.

"I need a moment," she said.

I nodded and she left. I settled in to watch the clock. After five minutes, I got up and walked down a carpeted hallway. To my left was a kitchen full of polish and stainless steel, then an open door that led to a bedroom. I stuck my head in and saw a tangle of sheets, but nothing else. On the other side of the hall were a bathroom and another door. I took out my gun and nudged the door with my foot.

"Come in, Mr. Kelly."

I pushed all the way in. Marie Perry was sitting behind a large old desk, staring at the rain streaming down a dark set of double-paned windows.

"This is Ray's desk," she said.

I sat down opposite her.

"My God, you took out your gun."

"It would be better if I could see your hands."

"Is it as serious as all that?"

"You tell me, ma'am."

She raised her hands slowly and placed them flat on the desk. "Better?"

I slipped my gun back into its holster. "Talk to me, Ms. Perry."

"What would you like to know?"

"Why are we in here?"

"This is Ray's room. Everything in here belongs to him."

"I assume the FBI's been through it all."

"With a fine-tooth comb. I insisted they ship it all back when they were done. His car's out in the garage. I haven't driven it since the day of the sentencing, but I keep it anyway."

"I'm right, aren't I, Ms. Perry?"

"About what?"

"The elevator. Ray's disappearance. Eddie Ward."

"If you're asking if I helped my husband avoid spending the best part of his life in jail, the answer is yes, I did."

Her whiskey sat on the desk. She reached for it, but thought better. "Those charges were a sham, Mr. Kelly. A political witch hunt. Ray didn't pressure people for donations. For Chrissakes, we had people lining up to give us cash."

"Where is he, Ms. Perry?"

"I don't know."

"I don't believe you."

"I didn't think you would." She slipped her hands beneath the desk again. I reached for my piece, and she froze. "I'm getting something out of my bag. It's not a gun. And you might find it instructive."

I nodded. "Go ahead."

She took out a long white envelope and placed it between us. Her first name was scrawled across the front.

"What is it?" I said.

"Ray gave me this on the morning he disappeared. Step-by-step instructions. What I had to do to get him out of the courthouse. What I needed to do after."

I reached for the envelope. Her voice stopped me. "Ray's dead, Mr. Kelly. Been dead for a while. He said it was easier that way."

CHAPTER 21

Exactly how did Ray get dead?" I said.

"Read the letter. It's all in there."

She got up and left. I sat behind Ray's desk and read. He didn't give up the big picture. Just specific directions for his wife. The elevator scam worked pretty much as I thought. Eddie Ward was in the car when Marie looked in. He took the elevator back up to the third floor, then walked down to ground level and waited for the cops to find him. By that time, Ray was long gone. He didn't give any indication in the letter where he was going. The closest he came was on the last page.

> My lawyer tells me the feds are going to try and fit me with a monitoring bracelet until I report to prison. I can't risk that. So it's got to be the courthouse. Today. Once I'm gone, there'll be a lot of scrutiny and threats. The government can't touch you. Not if you follow my instructions and stick to

> `the script. Don't worry about Eddie. He'll be taken care of. As for the rest, I know you can make a life out of it. Not in Chicago, maybe, but there are other places. Other dreams. Go after them. And forget about me. As far as you're concerned, Marie, I'm dead. At least for now. It hasn't been a perfect marriage, so maybe this is a blessing. I wish things could have been different, but we both know that wasn't in the cards. I'm sorry. Love, Ray.`

I heard a footfall in the hall outside. She was at the door.

"Finished?"

"Why do you have your coat on?"

"I assume we're going down to the police station."

"Why would we do that?"

"To give my statement. There's nothing in that letter that's going to lead them to Ray. And I don't know where he is, so that's another dead end. I'm sorry to steal your thunder, but I'd rather the police hear it directly from me."

"Sit down, Ms. Perry."

"I suspect 'Marie' is fine at this point."

"Sit down."

She took the seat I'd been in and waited, her smile shivering in its newfound vulnerability.

"You seem almost happy," I said.

"I'm just ready to move on."

"That's what your husband advises."

"Ray could be calculating when he needed to be."

I tapped the letter. "He says in here that Eddie's gonna be 'taken care of.' You know what that means?"

"I assume he'd be paid."

"So Ray had cash?"

She blinked. "I don't know."

"Why start lying now, Marie?"

"I'm not lying."

"You helped Ray either because you still love him, in which case all this talk about a marriage of convenience is just that. Talk."

"Or?"

"Or you helped him for some other reason."

"And you think it's about money?"

"Sorry, but it's just how things usually work. Either way, you're not telling me everything."

"You know as much as I do, Mr. Kelly. And sitting here staring at each other isn't going to change that."

"Fine," I said and got up.

"Are we going to the police?"

"We're going to see a friend."

"I didn't think we had any mutual friends."

"He's not my friend. He's yours. An electrician named Eddie Ward."

CHAPTER 22

Beatrice cracked the door as I tiptoed by. I gave her my best grin. She took one look and ducked back inside. One floor up, the door to Eddie Ward's apartment was exactly as I'd left it—broken. Marie hadn't said a word on the ride over and didn't seem surprised to be here. I wondered if she already knew what we'd find inside. I took out my gun and pushed the door open. The place hadn't changed a bit. I knelt and touched a finger to the layer of gray grit on the floor. I realized now what I should have seen then. It was cement dust. In the back of the apartment, the bedroom was still empty. I checked the closets and looked under the bed. Then I stripped off the blankets and sheets, but couldn't find any sign of the dust. Marie watched me from the doorway. Across from the bedroom was Eddie's only bathroom. At the very back of the bathroom was a claw-foot tub closed off by a shower curtain. I'd ignored the tub on my first visit. Now, I approached it and parted the shower curtain with the barrel of my gun. Someone had turned Eddie Ward's tub into a concrete paperweight.

I pulled out my phone and took a picture. Then I called Rodriguez.

We sat in the living room and waited for Rodriguez to show. Marie Perry's eyes kept dancing toward the back of the apartment. For the first time since I'd met her, she seemed truly nervous.

"Who did you call?" she said.

"A detective buddy of mine. I told him I needed a half hour."

"Why?"

"Because I wanted to give you time to get out of here."

"What if I don't want to leave?"

"The tub back there has been filled with concrete, Marie. When they break it open, they're gonna find Eddie Ward inside."

"You think so?"

"I'm sure of it. What I don't know is how he got there. And whether you had anything to do with it."

"I didn't even know the man."

"He helped you engineer Ray's escape. That made him a liability."

"If you believe that, then I'm a murderer. Setting aside the question of how I would maneuver a man into a tub full of concrete and why I would select that method to kill anyone, what's the motive behind letting me go?"

"Honestly?"

"Isn't honesty and trust the basis of this wonderful relationship we seem to have struck?"

"I don't believe you're a killer. Not yet anyway." I looked at my watch. "My friend's gonna be here soon. Head out the back and catch a cab. I'll call you once we crack open the tub."

I walked her through Eddie's kitchen to the back porch. She slipped down the stairs and moved quickly across a patchwork of Chicago alleys. The rain had tapered to a fine mist, and her hair glowed under the damp steam of the streetlights. I watched until she disappeared. Then I went back inside and waited. Rodriguez showed up ten minutes later.

"You clean up whatever you didn't want me to see?"

"You're better off not knowing."

"You think I'm complaining? Where is it?"

"In here." I led him to the bathroom and leaned up against the door frame. Rodriguez crouched close to the tub and studied it.

"How heavy is this thing?"

I shrugged. "You worried it's gonna go through the floor?"

"That's all I need."

"It'll be all right."

"This building's a piece of crap. What makes you think the floor can handle a tub full of concrete?"

I studied the gray surface. Smooth, flat, and hard. A professional job in more ways than one.

"We're gonna find Eddie in there," I said.

"Your electrician, I know. And you think it somehow connects back to Ray Perry?"

"There's a bigger picture here, Vince."

"Do me a favor and keep it to yourself."

"The boulder that crushed Paul Goggin's car wasn't a boulder at all. It was a slab of concrete." I crouched down and rapped the top of the tub. "Just like this one here."

"You already gave me that theory."

"It had to be at least a couple of guys who did Goggin. With some serious muscle and a plan."

"What kind of plan?"

"Someone follows Goggin in his car. Coordinates with the guys on the overpass so they get the timing right."

"You're reaching."

"You don't think that kid killed Goggin. You're too good a cop for that."

"What would you like me to do?"

"Let's go outside."

We walked out to the porch, wiped down a couple of chairs Eddie had stashed out there, and sat down. Rodriguez lit a cigarette. I'd grabbed a Coke out of the fridge.

"Someone's tying up loose ends," I said and popped open the soft drink.

"Chicago. City of loose ends." Rodriguez took a drag and blew smoke into the night.

"They also wanted to send a message. That's why they used the cement. First on Goggin. Then on Eddie."

"And who, exactly, are 'they'?"

"The guys who make a living in cement. Beacon Limited."

Rodriguez stared up at a starless sky and chuckled. "You're crazy."

"They donated four million dollars to Ray during his last year in office. More than fifteen million total. Spread out over four or five companies."

"So what. Beacon's been doing highway jobs in this state for thirty years."

"Yeah, but they hit the jackpot once Ray moved into the mansion."

"Hence, the fifteen mil." Rodriguez took another drag and flicked the butt over the railing. We both watched the trail of red sparks flare and die as they fell. Then I told the detective about my trip to the job site on the Eisenhower Expressway.

"So you're telling me you shot one of Beacon's security goons?"

"If he hasn't filed a report, maybe not. The point is they came after me. And there has to be a reason."

"Beyond the fact you were trespassing?"

"You don't see it?"

"I see it. You think Beacon was involved somehow in Ray Perry's disappearance. Why? You have no idea. And now they're burying people in bathtubs full of concrete and dropping hunks of the stuff on cars, presumably to cover their tracks. Sorry, Kelly, but I'm not buying. Now, answer me a question. Who did you hustle out of here before I came in?"

"Why would you think that?"

Rodriguez shook his head.

"What are you gonna do about the tub?" I said.

"I'm gonna call in a team. Break it open and see what we see. Pleasant way to spend the rest of my night."

"Here's something else to pass the time." I unfolded the police report Elena Ramirez had given me and handed it over.

"What's this?" the detective said.

"The guy in this report is a Chicago cop. I met his daughter the other day. Not the one listed in the report. His youngest, Elena."

Rodriguez glanced up, then kept reading.

"Elena says her father put a gun to her oldest sister's head after she told him she was gonna have a baby. Police whitewashed it as an accidental discharge of a weapon."

"This was four years ago. What do you want me to do?"

"Elena's sixteen and pregnant. She believes the old man might go ahead and pull the trigger this time around."

"And you think she's right?"

"I think I don't want to find out."

Rodriguez held up the report. "Can I keep this?"

"Sure."

"Okay. Clear out of here. I've got to call in a team and dig out Eddie."

"So you think it's Eddie, too?"

"It's Eddie. Probably owed the wrong guy some money. Now, take off. And next time you find a tub full of concrete, do me a favor and lose my number. And Kelly?"

"What?"

"If you're serious about Beacon, bring me some evidence. A motive wouldn't hurt either."

CHAPTER 23

Evidence and motive can be hard to come by, which is why I found myself hiking up onto a highway overpass at three-thirty in the morning. Jack O'Donnell had insisted we meet at the same Beacon job site I'd visited a week earlier, only this time the site was wrapped in darkness. I took out a nightscope and scanned the construction area. The place looked deserted. The scope was equipped with a thermal-imaging lens that told me all of the engines in the cars and trucks were cold. I slipped the scope back in my pocket and stared down at the Ike. The highway uncoiled like a jeweled serpent, stretching west toward the flatlands of Schaumberg and back into the heart of the city. A semi thumped past in a rush of wind and rubber. I walked back across the overpass, got in my car, and drove three exits east. Jack O'Donnell's blue SUV was waiting.

O'Donnell eased through the labyrinth of construction cones and pulled up to a fence emblazoned with a Hi-Top Construction logo. "If anyone asks what we're doing here, you let me talk."

"Fine."

He pulled a thermos of coffee from under his seat. "You want some?"

"No thanks."

"Suit yourself." O'Donnell poured himself a cup and sipped. Outside, sodium lamps were mounted on thick poles strung along the perimeter of the work site. The lamps threw chunks of hard white light on concrete dividers and silent lumps of machinery. Beyond that, the darkness was absolute.

"The first crew's scheduled to get here at five," O'Donnell said. "We'll be long gone by then." He was still a young man, in his early forties, with a small square head, anxious hairline, and quick, angled features. He flicked a hand at the world beyond his windshield and sighed. "Want to tell me why you care about this stuff?"

"It might tie into a case I'm working."

"What sort of case?"

"I got hired by a guy . . ."

"What guy?"

"Actually I don't even know if it is a guy. Might be a woman."

"You're a private investigator and you don't know who hired you?"

I described the e-mail I'd gotten, followed by the adrenaline shot to my bank account. O'Donnell whistled. Low and smart. "Sounds like my kind of client. Why does he want you to find Perry?"

"No idea."

"And that doesn't bother you?"

"Not yet."

"How do you think I can help?"

"Tell me about Beacon Limited."

"The roads of Illinois are paved in red and white."

"Excuse me?"

"Those are the colors Beacon uses for all its subsidiaries. Red and white." O'Donnell cranked open the driver's-side door and flicked on a flashlight. "Come on. Let's take a walk."

The entrance to the site had a gate that was latched, but not locked. O'Donnell didn't seem surprised and eased it open. The highway curved gently to the left. I could see the reporter's breath in the predawn cold and hear the scrape of his boots in the gravel. We walked for about a hundred yards and stopped.

"Six years ago, this road got a face-lift," O'Donnell said.

"I remember. Edens, Kennedy. They all got face-lifts."

"Let's stick with the Ike."

"Fine."

"You know how a road's built?"

I shook my head.

"The old highway had twelve inches of gravel, called a sub-base, covered over by four inches of asphalt and ten inches of concrete. That's twenty-six inches deep. Not enough for today's traffic. Beacon's people proposed laying in a new surface—twenty-four inches of sub-base, six inches of asphalt, and fourteen of concrete. That's forty-four inches, as thick and sturdy as any piece of highway ever built in this state. Great, right?"

I nodded.

"Then why are we six years in and it's falling apart? This way."

We cut between two dividers and walked past a couple of dump trucks. They were painted in violent shades of red and black and had EAGLE CEMENT, another Beacon subsidiary, printed across their doors in white block letters.

"The Eisenhower project began in 2006," O'Donnell said.

"Ray's first year in the mansion. Finished up in the winter of 2008. Beacon initially estimated the cost at eight hundred million dollars. The final price tag was closer to one-point-four billion. Springfield kicked, but Perry rammed it through the legislature anyway. Here, take a look at this."

O'Donnell set his flashlight on the ground and squatted beside a gray tarp that covered a hundred yards of road. He removed a couple of pegs and peeled back the covering. Two parallel cracks, each about five feet long and a couple of inches wide, ran side by side down the middle of the road. O'Donnell peeled back the tarp a little farther. The cracks cobwebbed into smaller fractures and split off in a dozen different directions.

"Beacon claims this is nothing," O'Donnell said. "Just surface cracks that are easily patched."

"And is it?"

O'Donnell pulled a steel tape measure from his vest and slid it into one of the main fissures. "This one runs almost ten inches deep. Halfway to the sub-base. It's a major flaw and an indication the road's falling apart." O'Donnell snapped his tape measure shut. "As we speak, Beacon has seven different 'patching operations' they're doing on the Ike." O'Donnell stood and looked back behind us. "It's gonna be getting light soon. Let's get back to the car."

We didn't say a word on the walk back. O'Donnell climbed behind the wheel. I got in the passenger's side. For the first time I noticed a child's booster seat locked into the seat behind me. We drove back to my car, parked on a dead-end street bellied up next to the highway. O'Donnell took out a laptop and fired it up.

"What's your e-mail?"

I gave it to him.

"I'm sending you information on three crashes that happened on the Ike. Six fatalities, total. Including three kids."

O'Donnell turned around the laptop so I could see a picture of a ten-year-old girl in her school uniform.

"I visited two of the accident sites myself," O'Donnell said. "They'd already patched up most of the road, but I was able to get a look at the damage underneath."

"And?"

"I saw the same cracks you saw tonight. A road essentially coming apart at the seams."

"And you think it caused these crashes?"

"Clean driving records. No evidence of drugs or drinking. No bad weather. I can't prove it, but, yes, I'm convinced it was the road that killed them."

I scrolled through a list of the articles. Then I returned to the picture of the kid. "You're going to send this stuff to me?"

"I already did."

"How about evidence? Did you take any photos of the accident sites when you visited them?"

"I shot some videotape, but it won't help."

"Why not?"

"It's not conclusive. Not even close."

"Can I see the tapes?"

O'Donnell glanced out the window at the heavy chain-link fence that separated us from the expressway. "Let's wait on that."

"Fine. So, how did they do it?"

"Do what?"

"Cheat the system? Spend a billion dollars and build a substandard highway without anyone catching on?"

"It's not as hard as you think. In this case, they probably did a couple of things. First, there are the state's weigh scales. Trucks filled with cement would be weighed as they left Beacon plants in the morning. The state would then be billed for raw materials based on those readings."

"Beacon messed with the scales?"

"Most likely they rigged the computers that recorded the weights. Five tons of material get recorded as six, and the state gets overbilled. Every single day. Every single truck. Adds up pretty quick."

"What else?"

"They cheat on their mix. A contractor has certain specs he's supposed to follow in creating asphalt and concrete mixes. If they skimp on the recipe, throw in a little more sand, too much water, the mix gets compromised. And the contractor saves money."

"How much money?"

O'Donnell chuckled. "On a project like this? The final price tag to the state was roughly one-point-four billion. Based on the quality of work I've seen, I wouldn't be surprised if Beacon skimmed fifteen, twenty percent of that."

"That's almost three hundred million dollars."

"And that's just the Ike."

"Why haven't you written a story on any of this?"

O'Donnell jerked his head toward the child's seat in the back. "My youngest was three years old last month. You think she deserves a dad? 'Cuz I do."

"It's like that, huh?"

"I first got onto Beacon when I was with the *Trib.* My editor killed every investigative piece I ever pitched. One night he took me out for a drink. Said he wanted to talk about my work. So we had our drink. Actually, a few drinks. Then he pulled out an envelope. Inside was a picture of my oldest. Six, seven years old at the time. She was holding the hand of a man and smiling. The man was cut off at the shoulders so I couldn't see his face." O'Donnell's voice was even, but there were the faintest tracings of pink in his face and a froth of spittle at the corner of his mouth. "I grabbed my boss by the throat and was about to put my fist through his teeth. Job be damned. He pulls out a second photo. His kid. Same age as mine. Same guy holding her hand. My boss told me we wouldn't run anything on Beacon. Now or ever. Not if we loved our kids. I agreed. We had another drink and never talked about it again." O'Donnell pulled the thermos out from under his seat and unscrewed the cap. "You sure you don't want some?"

I nodded and he poured us each a cup of coffee. I took a sip. It was hot and strong.

"Why are you here, Jack?"

"You're supposed to be a hard man. And you don't have any family. I figured maybe you could do something about it."

"Who owns Beacon?"

"If I knew, I'd tell you."

"Can you give me anything else?"

"I've already given you too much."

"How about the tapes you made of the roads?"

"I'll think about that."

I took out one of my business cards and stuck it on the dash. "Thanks, Jack."

"Good luck. And don't call me again."

I climbed out of O'Donnell's SUV and watched him drive away. Then I got in my car and headed back to the job site. I figured I still had some time and wanted to get another look under that tarp. So I got out and picked my way across the work zone. There was a fresh wind at my back, and the first fingers of sunlight brushed the highway in delicate shades of blush. I found the section O'Donnell had led me to and walked a bit farther. Then I crouched down and peeled back the thick canvas. The cracks here were wider and deeper. I took out a small flashlight I'd brought with me and positioned it so it lit up one of the largest fault lines. I was about to snap a photo with my phone when I heard the hard crunch of gravel behind me. I reached for my gun and looked back. Just in time to see the dark shape of a shovel dropping out of a sky frosted in pink.

CHAPTER 24

The water was cold and dirty, forcing its way up my nose and sluicing between my teeth. I knew better than to struggle. If the person leaning on the back of my head wanted to drown me, my resistance would only accelerate the process. And why drown me in the first place? A gun was easier. The hand seemed to read my mind as I was pulled free of the bucket. I coughed and retched. Someone dragged me to a chair and cuffed me. Then a black bag went over my head. I never saw the shovel coming this time.

I woke up strapped to a chair. My hands were stretched out, palms down, fingers spread and secured to a table made of grained wood. There was some dim light behind me and a pockmarked wall in front. I could hear breathing and guessed there were at least two of them. They smelled like smokers. One stepped out where I could see him. It was Iron Belly. He carried the shovel in both hands.

"Maybe we should put the bag over your head?" I said.

Iron Belly rammed the shovel, blade first, into my stomach. If I'd eaten anything, I would have lost it. As it was, I just retched some more and spit on the floor.

"Who was with you at the job site tonight?" Iron Belly's voice was low and guttural, like a metal burr being buzzed flat by a bandsaw.

"I was by myself."

Another shot to the gut. Not as bad this time. But when I retched, I saw leavings of blood in my saliva.

"Who was with you?"

"Fuck you."

Iron Belly raised the shovel again, then paused. The other man in the room walked out onto the small, sullen stage and took a seat across from me.

"I'm enjoying the hell out of this," Bones McIntyre said. "How about you?"

I spat in his general direction. Iron Belly made another move with the shovel, but Bones waved him off.

"I'm surprised you'd let me see your face," I said.

"That's because you don't understand how we work." Bones pulled out one of his cigars and rolled it between a thumb and forefinger. Then he took out a silver cutter on a chain and clipped off the end.

"Why don't you explain it to me?" I said.

Bones crinkled his forehead in surprise. "I already tried."

"Try again."

"Maybe a little history would help." He struck a match and sucked up the yellow flame in a long, cool draw. The room filled with the rich smell of burning tobacco. Bones eased back in his chair and picked a piece of cigar wrapper off his spotted tongue. "The whole thing started in the late eighties. The powers in this town decided they needed their own little cash cow. A slice of an anonymous industry they could fleece without anyone being the wiser. So they picked highway construction. And they created Beacon Limited." Another draw and a ribbon of blue smoke spiraled over my head. "All the heavy hitters bought in. City, county, state. We built our fix into the DNA of the system, cooked the amounts we planned on skimming right into the state budget. I like to call it the Chicago annuity. Hell, we've been doing it so long, it almost seems legal." The old politician chuckled and laid his cigar down so the ash hung, pregnant, over the side of the table. Then he tipped forward and tapped me on the forearm. "That's why someone like you could never make a case against us. If you did, you'd be taking it to a cop whose boss or boss's boss is part of Beacon. Same thing with all the major prosecutors in the state and half the judges on the bench. The thing would go nowhere. And whoever you gave it to would have their career snuffed. Maybe worse."

"No one could have things locked up that tight."

"We're very discreet. Our interests are narrowly defined. And we only exercise our muscle when those interests are directly affected."

"I don't believe it."

Bones turned to look at Iron Belly. "He doesn't believe it." Back to me. "I could put a bullet in your head. Leave the gun here with my prints on it and walk away clean. I guess that would make my case. Of course you'd be dead, so the 'I told you so' might feel a little hollow."

"And what's stopping you?"

"First smart thing you've said all night. There's one person we don't control. And that's Ray Perry. You're gonna help us with that." Bones walked behind me and came back to the table with an iPad. "Surprised? Old fuck like me. Rotary phone, all that shit. What do I know about technology? Nothing, really. They cue the stuff up, and I just play it. This one I've played a half-dozen times."

Bones flipped the iPad around and hit a button. A video rolled. The camera was somewhere in Rachel Swenson's bedroom. I closed my eyes, but it didn't matter. I could hear the soft groans and oiled squeak of bedsprings I knew all too well.

"She's had a couple of cowboys in there since you." Bones's voice had dropped to a hazy whisper. "This one's a trader down at the Merc. We paid him to make the tape. He did your girl for nothing."

Iron Belly snickered, and I knew somewhere in my brain he'd just bought himself a bullet. Bones was a given.

"We'll take the judge whenever we want," he said. "Ruin her professionally, financially, or maybe just have her raped and killed in that pretty fucking graystone of hers. We'll videotape that, too, and send it to you. Open your eyes."

I did. The iPad had gone to a merciful black. Bones scraped his chair closer and fixed me with a slitted stare. "Tell Ray I want my money. If he gets it to me, I'll forget about him. And you."

"What money?"

"Tell him."

"I don't know where Ray is."

Bones's smile was a razor. In its bloody arc, I caught a glimpse of the awful price paid for power. "Just tell him, Kelly. And keep your fingers out of other people's business. We'll all get along fine."

Fear spiked a claw in my gut as Bones McIntyre rose out of his chair. Iron Belly stood just behind him. The shovel had been replaced by a hatchet. My eyes flew to my hands, naked and spread, each finger separated and secured to the rough wood with a small metal clamp. Somewhere in my head a door closed and I knew, whatever happened, things would never be the same. I looked up again at Iron Belly, gaze flat as a sledgehammer. In one movement he raised the hatchet and swung it down, through a crust of nail, tissue, blood, and nerve, until the sharp blade bit into the ragged wood and stuck there. I might have screamed. I'm sure I screamed, but it was drowned out by the roar in my ears. Then my eyes rolled back in my head, and my world went white with pain.

CHAPTER 25

I looked down at the brown Jewel bag puddled with blood and wrapped around my left hand. Then I looked up. The gun seemed more like a cannon in the hands of a ten-year-old. He had a finger curled around the trigger and the business end pointed at my head.

"That's my gun." The words were torn from my lips by a howl of wind, and I wondered if I'd really said anything at all. Apparently I had, because the kid gave me his best fifth-grade smile. "Got you on the red beam, Casper." The kid tucked the howitzer into the belt of his jeans and swaggered off down the street.

I leaned back on the wooden steps and stared up at a purple sky dipped in hues of orange and red. They'd dragged me out of the cellar and thrown me into a car. I remembered some shapes and a large jolt. Rough hands at my neck, the smell of sour sweat and cigarettes, cold air and cracked pavement. Then, the kid. I looked down the street and back up it. I'd been dumped on the steps of a building that was more bones than flesh. The rest of the block was a similar parade of skeletons, black sockets where windows should be; others boarded up and nailed shut. On a corner, two street signs stood naked in the newborn light. I was at Fifteenth and Drake in Lawndale. Score one for the home team. I felt the edge of my mobile in my jacket. Score another for the good guys. I took the phone out with my right hand and fumbled to make a call. I knew I was on the jagged edge of shock. Knew if I succumbed the next passerby would take my money and my phone. Or maybe the kid would come back with my gun and finish the job. I hit a button and waited. Rodriguez's voice came alive at the other end of the line.

"It's six in the morning."

"I'm at Fifteenth and Drake."

"What the fuck are you doing out there?"

"Nothing good."

"You don't sound so hot."

"I'm not. Can you get here?"

"Sure."

"Bring a first-aid kit."

A pause. "Are you hurt?"

I glanced at the soggy Jewel bag. "Probably."

"An ambulance might be quicker."

"No ambulance." I looked up. The kid wasn't back. But his older brother was. "I gotta go, Vince. Just get down here."

I cut the call and laid the phone down on the step beside me. He was maybe sixteen, lean with fine features and hard, bright eyes—in another world, the savvy point guard on someone's basketball team. He wore a black leather coat that fell almost to his knees and pulled my gun from somewhere out of one of its folds.

"You give this to Shorty?"

"He took it from me." I held up the bag of blood to indicate my problem. His eyes flared, then went back to calculating.

"Who fucked wit' you?"

"No one you know."

He still had my gun in his hand and tapped it against his leg as he thought things through. "What else you got in your pockets?"

I gave him the phone and some cash. I wasn't gonna give him my ID and plastic. Let him search for that. He counted the money and powered the phone on and off. Then he pocketed it.

"You a cop?"

I shook my head. "I work with one. That was him I was talking to."

"What's his name?"

"Rodriguez."

"Vince?"

"You know him?"

"Tell him LJ said 'What up?' " LJ stuck my gun back in one of his long pockets and wandered off. Fifteen minutes later, Rodriguez pulled to the curb. I slipped into the front seat.

"LJ says hey."

"LJ?"

"One of your buddies down here. He just lifted my gun and phone."

"I'll get 'em back. What happened to your hand?"

I looked over at Rodriguez. His face rippled like a bedsheet pegged to a clothesline in a summer storm. The air around him stretched and snapped, reality smoking and fraying at the seams.

"Get me to a hospital," I said and slumped back against the seat. The car began to move. My head slid until it hit the passenger's-side window. The next thing I felt was a cool hand on my forehead, the squeak of rubber wheels on tile, and the sharp tug of a syringe as it bit into my arm.

CHAPTER 26

I was in a hospital bed, my left hand wrapped in gauze and resting on my chest. My head seemed a little spongy, and my throat was parched. Otherwise, I didn't feel so bad. A door opened, and a nurse came in.

"You're awake?" She was young, with cropped black hair and skin dusted in cinnamon.

"I guess so," I said. "Still a little groggy. Where am I?"

"You're at Northwestern Memorial, and you've been out for about four hours. My name's Janice, by the way."

"Hi, Janice. Michael." I held up the wrapped club they'd left me as a hand. "So, what's the damage?"

Janice pulled a blood-pressure cuff off the wall and wound it around my arm. "The doctor will give you the details, but it wasn't too bad."

"Really, 'cuz this bandage looks pretty big."

"You were a little shocky when you came in, so they stabilized you. The injury itself was to the very top part of your pinkie." She held up her own and pinched off a thin sliver of skin above the nail. "About this much. And the entire nail. No surgery necessary. Just some stitches. Take the antibiotics and pain pills, and you should be good to go."

"Huh."

"You were pretty lucky. What happened, anyway?"

"Gardening shears."

"At six a.m.?"

"Pruning roses at dawn. Calms the nerves."

"You came in with a detective."

"Is that what he told you?"

"He left when they were stitching you up. Came back an hour later and dropped this off." Janice unwrapped the cuff and pointed to my smartphone sitting on a small table by the bed. "He said to tell you he had the rest of your stuff."

"Thanks, Janice."

"Sure." She checked an IV drip they had me hooked up to. "You want something for the pain?"

"I thought you'd never ask."

She returned with a small cup of pills. I took them without any water. I didn't have a lot of pain but figured it would come soon enough. Janice was watching me closely.

"Are you going to tell me what really happened?"

"You didn't buy the gardening shears?"

"No."

"If I told you the real story, you'd believe it even less. What's the stuff you're pumping into my arm?"

"Just some antibiotics. You'll have to stay here until a doctor sees you."

"Not a problem."

"Might be a few hours."

"I'm beat. Just want to get some sleep."

"Good." She plumped a few pillows, turned out the lights, and left. I waited a couple of minutes, tugged the IV out of my arm, and climbed out of bed. My clothes were hanging in a closet. I got dressed with some difficulty, found some tape and gauze in a cabinet, and stuffed them under my coat. Then I tucked my bad hand in my pocket, walked down the corridor, and hit the elevator. The hospital lobby was mostly empty. I walked over to a Starbucks and ordered a black coffee. In the gift shop, I bought a bottle of extra-strength Tylenol and took a couple. Then I pushed through the revolving doors and walked up to Michigan Avenue. I was in a cab heading north when I pulled out my phone and punched in Rodriguez's number.

CHAPTER 27

"I need you to do me a favor," I said.

"What was last night? Where are you anyway?"

"In a cab."

"They let you out?"

"Sort of. Listen, I need someone to watch Rachel."

"Why don't we talk about what happened to your hand?"

"We will, but I need someone watching Rachel now."

"Fine, I'll get someone."

"No cops."

"Why not?"

"It's not safe," I said. "Use someone private."

"Okay. Someone private."

"Her apartment might be bugged. It needs to be swept. And she can't know anything about it. Money's not a problem."

"Big spender. Let me make a call. I got your gun, by the way."

"I know. Janice told me."

"Who's Janice?"

"Never mind."

"How's the hand?"

"My finger. It's fine. Just a few stitches. What did you pull out of Eddie's bathtub?"

"What we thought."

"Eddie?"

"Took a slug in the forehead before he went in. My boss will sit on it for a week. Then he wants an arrest and doesn't much care who. Want some free advice?"

"Not really."

"Take a vacation. Enjoy your hundred K. And forget about Ray Perry."

"I'll call you." I cut the line just as we rolled to a stop on Broadway. I paid the cabbie and went up to my office. My first call was to Jack O'Donnell. I got his voice mail and left a message. Then I sat back and stared out the window at traffic. I could feel the pain building in my forearm and squeezed the bandage lightly. Bones could have taken a finger. Hell, he could have taken the hand. But he just wanted to hurt. Enough to scare. Enough to deliver a message. I thought about Rachel and wondered how long that movie would be playing inside my head. My phone buzzed and the e-mail icon blinked. I tapped it and read the message.

There's an extra 10k in the account for medical expenses.

I typed with one finger.

Who am I talking to?

Your client.

I need a name.

A pause, then I typed another line.

Am I talking to Ray?

The answer came quickly.

Yes.

Why did you hire me?

Beacon.

Did you take their money?

Not important. Focus on my wife. She's in danger.

I thought about that, then typed again.

Why did she help you get out of the courthouse?

Another pause, then a response.

Not important. Your apartment is bugged. Video, audio.
Laptop/phone at home probably not secure. Office okay.
Good-bye.

I stared at the last message for half a minute. Then I went down the hall to the bathroom and locked the door. Every instinct told me to find the bugs in my apartment and rip them out. Right now, however, they were a potential lead. Which meant they'd stay in place. And I'd live with it. I turned on the water and looked at my face in the mirror. Carefully, I peeled off a row of butterfly stitches they'd used to close up a gash in my eyebrow. It bled a little but stopped pretty quickly. I moved on to my hand, unwinding the bandage slowly. The top half of my finger was black with bruising and flat, a row of stitches marching along the top and down one side. I touched the finger lightly but couldn't feel anything so I tried to bend it. The pain shot up my arm, froze my elbow, and exploded in my shoulder. I leaned over the sink and took a deep breath. After a minute or so, I stood up and rewrapped the hand, taping my pinkie and ring fingers together so the rest of my hand was free. Then I splashed some cold water on my face and wiped it dry with a paper towel. I unlocked the bathroom door and walked back down the hallway, wondering if Ray Perry had really been on the other end of that e-mail exchange. And if so, what did he want? I turned the corner to find Bones McIntyre waiting outside my office. He had a pencil in hand and was reading a *Tribune*.

"Kelly, what's an eight-letter word for 'morally bankrupt'?"

"'Politics.' I'm guessing you want to come in?"

CHAPTER 28

Bones followed me into the office. "How's the hand?"

"The hand's fine." I walked behind my desk, cracked open the window, and sat down. The gun was five feet away, in the bottom right-hand drawer. My fingers itched for it, and I could feel the heat pouring off my skin. I blinked away the moment and softened my face. "What do you want?"

Bones walked across to my bookcase and ran his fingers along the spines.

"Your daughter did the same thing when she was here."

"Really? What did she pick out?"

"I'll let her tell you."

Bones chuckled and selected a volume. "*The Twelve Labors of Hercules.*"

"You read it?"

"Believe it or not, I did. Long time ago." He opened the book and turned a few pages. "The Hydra. Snake with all the heads, right?"

"Yep. Hercules cut off one, and two grew back."

"Must have made things tough." Bones found a chair and settled in it.

"Why are you here?" I said.

"The Hydra." He held up the book. "You can't beat it."

"Hercules did."

"You ain't no fucking Hercules."

"I thought we covered this last night."

"We did, but I got to thinking. There was a look on your face when I mentioned the money."

"The money Ray Perry stole from you?"

"That's right. I could have sworn you didn't know what the fuck I was talking about."

"I don't."

"Son of a bitch if I don't believe you."

"I'm thrilled."

The old man let his eyes harden into polished chips of granite. "You want to listen to what I have to say? Or maybe next time we take the whole hand?"

I felt the city's breath hot on the back of my neck. Outside, a CTA bus groaned to a halt, and the door hissed open. "Go ahead."

"My daughter."

"I thought you two weren't close?"

"She's still my daughter."

"Okay. What about her?"

Bones walked back to the shelf, where he replaced the book. I waited until he sat back down again.

"Is she part of Beacon?" I said.

"Hardly."

"Then what?"

"Ray was in it," Bones said. "Every governor in the last twenty years has been in it. But Ray loved it. He pushed for more contracts, more work, more cash, more skim. That's why he rammed all those highway bills through Springfield. That was Ray all the way. Taking Beacon to the next level, he called it."

"What happened?"

"The investigation that put him in jail was a witch hunt. A federal thing that had nothing to do with us."

"But it disrupted things?"

"We told Ray to do his time, and we'd get some cash to Marie. Make sure he was comfortable inside."

"Ray didn't like that?"

"Ray took off with our money."

"How much are we talking about?"

"Sixty million."

I whistled despite myself.

"That's right," Bones said. "On the day he disappeared, so did the cash. From three separate accounts. We've been patient, hoping Ray would come to his senses and try to make a deal."

"How much does your daughter know?"

"That's the question. And the reason she's still alive. Some people think she might know about the money. If not, then maybe where Ray is."

"Doesn't sound like you believe that?"

"If she knew where the money was, why stick around Chicago?"

The old man had put his finger on it. Either Marie Perry knew nothing and was just another victim. Or she knew everything and was staying in the city to keep someone or something safe.

"There's another question, Bones."

"What's that?"

"Could you drop the hammer on your daughter if need be?"

He sat in the pale sunlight and blinked against the glare. His eyes were black hollows. His nose, once aristocratic, now just looked long and bony, reaching back into a forehead that ended in a few wisps of white hair slicked back over his skull. "My daughter's been dead to me for a long time, Kelly. Nothing's gonna change that."

"Do your pals at Beacon believe that? Because I don't."

Bones wrinkled his brow. "You realize the clock on this thing has just about run out?"

"What do you want from me?"

"Ray did some good work for us. I'd be willing to let him stay hidden and keep ten million for himself. Considering he's looking at thirty years in prison, I'd say that's a pretty good deal."

"Or he could stay hidden and keep all sixty."

"You want to get people killed, just keep on trucking."

"I already told you, I don't know where Ray is."

"Marie might."

"Why do you say that?"

"Because Ray would have reached out. Even if she wanted nothing to do with him, I could see the guy reaching out."

"And that's what you've been waiting for?"

"Talk to Marie. Tell her to convince Ray to take the deal. Then get her out of the city. If she doesn't want to play, tell her my hands are tied."

"That's it?"

"Let the rest of it go. Whatever you thought you saw last night on the Ike, forget about it. And consider yourself lucky to get away with a couple of stitches."

I took the gun out of the drawer and held it in my good hand. "The Hydra was a *female* serpent, Bones. She was so lethal that men who even walked in her tracks were poisoned and died."

"What the Christ does that mean?"

"It means I don't trust your daughter any more than I trust you. And I intend to take the whole family down if I have to. In fact, I look forward to it. Now, get out of my office before I put a bullet in you."

CHAPTER 29

I watched from the window as Bones McIntyre crossed Broadway and kept going. Then I leaned back in my chair, put my feet on the desk, and promptly fell asleep. When I woke up, it was almost four in the afternoon. My mouth was full of sand, and my hand was throbbing. I poured myself a glass of water and popped another handful of Tylenol. Then I picked up the phone and called Marie Perry. There was no answer on her cell or at home. I pulled out a red leather case from a cabinet behind my desk. Inside was a small tool kit and a dozen lock picks. I put the case in a duffel along with a pair of gloves, a roll of tape, and my gun. I was about to leave when the phone rang. I thought it might be Marie. Or maybe Jack O'Donnell returning my earlier call. I was close.

They'd left O'Donnell in his boxers, faceup on the bed. His eyes were open, one hand splayed out to the left, the other curled into a claw. The wound ran across his neck and plunged in a ragged line to the breastbone. The sheets and mattress on his bed looked like they'd been soaked through to the box spring. His skin was a slushy gray. I stacked the pictures in a pile and shoved them back across to Rodriguez. We were sitting in a Dunkin' Donuts on Irving Park just west of the Kennedy. O'Donnell lived in a one-bedroom walk-up three blocks south. The detectives working the scene had found my business card among his personal effects and put a call in to Rodriguez. He'd taken a quick look inside the apartment and decided he didn't want me anywhere near it. I couldn't blame him.

"The guy lived like shit," Rodriguez said and shoveled some sugar into a cup of black coffee. There was a plain doughnut beside it. "Did you know he was divorced?"

"I knew he had kids."

"She left him a couple of years back. Cleaned him out pretty good is what we're hearing. Anyway, she's devastated. Wants to know how this could have happened."

"And?"

Rodriguez broke off a piece of the doughnut and popped it in his mouth. "Been dead at least eight hours, maybe more. The official theory is a break-in."

"What did they take?"

"Hard to say. Why?"

"O'Donnell made some tapes of the patch-up jobs Beacon was doing on the highway."

"Didn't see any tapes."

"How about notes? Computer files?"

"Only thing in there was a nineteen-inch color TV, and that looked like it was busted. So O'Donnell *was* working with you?"

"He was with me out on the Ike last night but left before I got grabbed. I tried to call him today. Wanted to tell him to stay in a hotel."

"Yeah, well, he never got the message." Rodriguez slipped the crime-scene photos back into a folder and glanced reluctantly around the empty coffee shop. "Maybe it's time you told me the whole story on Beacon."

So I did, starting with O'Donnell's midnight tour of the Ike, working my way through the heart-to-heart with Bones, and ending with Iron Belly taking a small ax to my hand. By the time I'd finished, Vince was staring out the window at rush-hour traffic. I thought about O'Donnell and the picture of his little girl. Vince's voice floated in from somewhere.

"I can bring them in for questioning. Lean on Bones a little."

"What's the point? He claims they've got the system gamed. Your boss. Your boss's boss. All the way up."

"You believe him?"

"When he tells it, I believe him, yeah."

"So we just sit back and watch the bodies pile up?"

"No."

"Then what?"

"I think I know who hired me."

"Who?"

"Ray Perry."

"Ray Perry hired you to find Ray Perry?"

"He hired me to ask questions. Hit some pressure points."

"And Ray told you this himself?"

"I talked to him this morning."

"So you know where Ray is?"

"Not exactly, but that doesn't matter. He wants me to play a lone hand, and he's right. I need to go after Bones and Beacon where they're most vulnerable."

"And where's that?"

"Bones claims he's got no time for his daughter, but I don't buy it. In fact, I think it's all about her. I'm just not sure how. Did you find someone to watch Rachel?"

"They'll be there tonight."

"Drop me a line when they're in place."

Rodriguez nodded at the bandage on my hand. "How bad is it?"

"Not as bad as what O'Donnell caught."

"Go get some sleep."

"On my way."

I parked just down the block from Rachel's place. The engine ticked over, and the clock on my dashboard read 7:45. I turned on the radio, cracked the window, and watched the twisted light reflected in her windows. A pair of headlights swept by, and the past crept in like fog, clouding up the glass and covering my eyes in velvet. I used my good hand to wipe the windshield clean, and there she was, sitting on the edge of my old bathtub, one foot on the rolled rim, doing her nails and drinking a cup of tea. I watched as Rachel painted. Listened as she hummed. Soaked in the things that had a way of circling back, whether you wanted them to or not. Like the way she bit her lip just before she smiled. The way she smiled just before she laughed. The dead eyes that lived inside Jack O'Donnell's apartment. The past. It came in all shapes and flavors. I snapped my eyes open and shook my head. The clock on my dashboard read 9:23. Rodriguez was sitting beside me in his car. Slowly, he lowered the window.

"I didn't tell you to sleep on the street."

"I just closed my eyes for a second. How did you know I'd be here?"

The detective shrugged. "Lucky guess."

"Are your people in place?"

"They see you. You don't see them. Tomorrow, they'll go in and check out her place."

"Thanks, Vince. I owe you."

"You want to tell me how much danger she's in?"

"It's just a precaution."

"You gonna talk to her about it?"

"Not sure."

"You ever gonna talk to her?"

"Not sure about that either."

"Mature as hell, Kelly. Go home and go to bed." Rodriguez raised his window and pulled away. I watched for another hour, until the lights went out in Rachel Swenson's bedroom. Then I left.

CHAPTER 30

They found Ray Perry's body the next morning. I was in my office, drinking a cup of coffee and thinking about phoning Jack O'Donnell's ex-wife when the call came in. Rodriguez was en route and didn't have a lot of details. I got in my car and drove out to the Ambassador Motel, one of a string of rent-by-the hour dumps that populate a stretch of Lincoln Avenue just south of Devon. The parking lot was empty, save for a single squad car, a couple of county medical vans, and Rodriguez's unmarked unit. He was just getting out as I pulled up.

"You been inside?" I said.

The detective shook his head. "All I know is they got an anonymous tip on a body, and they've ID'd it as Ray. Manager says the room wasn't rented out."

"So someone broke in?"

"Looks that way."

"What about the press?"

"Caught a break there. The cop who took the call recognized Ray and kept it off the radio. Right now it's just a couple of uniforms, us, and the coroner. Let's go."

Rodriguez led me up a flight of steps, down a gangway, and past a bunch of closed doors.

"Who's keeping the other guests quiet?" I said.

"The owner told his patrons the cops were on their way. Maybe a few news cameras as well. Everyone cleared out pretty quick after that. Right here."

A single uniform stood sentry in front of room 235. He watched as we put on booties, masks, and gloves. Then we stepped inside. A medical team was working over the bed, taking pictures and talking quietly. Otherwise, there were just a couple of cops and us. A woman detached herself from the group and came over.

"Kelli Spencer from the coroner's office."

"Detective Rodriguez from Homicide. This is Michael Kelly. He's a PI who's been helping us look for the deceased."

We shook hands all around. All I could see of Spencer was a set of light blue eyes above her mask. And they seemed entertained as hell. I'd been around enough crime scenes to know Spencer had a secret. And she thought it was a pretty good one.

"Where are we at?" Rodriguez said.

"We've photographed the body and examined it."

"And?"

"Maybe you should take a look first. Then we can talk."

The small circle of folks around the bed parted as we approached. Ray Perry lay on his back. Wrinkled, gray, and dead. They'd stripped him down to his underwear and covered his hands and feet with plastic bags. A pair of chinos, a blue-and-white checked shirt, and black lace-up shoes sat in a pile at the foot of the bed. His hands, bags and all, were laid across his chest, and his mouth was set in an eternal pucker. The Ray I remembered wouldn't have liked that at all.

"How did he die?" Rodriguez said.

"That's the thing," Spencer said. One of her assistants leaned over to whisper in her ear. Spencer nodded, and the assistant left the room. Spencer turned back to us. "Best we can tell, Mr. Perry died of natural causes."

"What kind of natural causes?" I said.

"We won't know until we do a full autopsy, but I'd say massive organ failure, probably related to some form of cancer."

"Cancer?" Rodriguez glanced at me, then back to Spencer.

"Given the jaundice and general condition of the body, I'd guess leukemia. The blood work, of course, will tell us more, but that's my guess."

"How long's he been dead?" I said.

"A couple of days, at least. That's the other interesting thing. The temperature reading we got indicates the body has been refrigerated."

"So you don't think he died here?" Rodriguez said.

Spencer looked around. "Not unless this place doubles as a walk-in cooler. Of course, we'll know more when we do a complete autopsy."

"How long can you keep this quiet?" Rodriguez said.

"A few days, maybe a week, before we file a report. Is that what you want?"

"Probably. You ready to move the body?"

"Just about."

"All right, I'm gonna get a team in here to sweep the place for evidence. Let them get a look before you move him."

"Of course."

"Thanks, Doc."

We shook hands, and I got the feeling Dr. Spencer was still having a laugh at our expense. That was fine. Someone should. We walked back out onto the balcony. Rodriguez took a moment to examine the lock to the room.

"Take someone twenty seconds to jimmy this. They pull the car in below, carry him up in the middle of the night."

"No one's gonna be looking out the windows in this place," I said, staring down a row of silver doorknobs.

Rodriguez grunted his assent and stripped off his mask and gloves. Then he leaned up against the chipped iron railing and studied me in the shaded light. "You want to explain something to me?"

"What's that?"

"How is it that Ray Perry's been dead for two days, but he was talking to you yesterday?"

"It was more like an e-mail."

"An e-mail. That's not really like talking to someone, is it, Kelly?"

I glanced back through the open door, at the body on the bed. "Apparently not."

Rodriguez was about to respond when a black Lexus pulled into the lot below.

"Vince."

"What?"

I nodded as Marie Perry got out of the car, dark sunglasses dropped over her eyes. Rodriguez cursed under his breath and met her at the top of the stairs, detective star out and in his right hand.

"Ms. Perry."

"I was told they found my husband's body?"

"Yes, but it would be best to ID him at the morgue."

Marie took off the sunglasses. "I've already talked to your boss. I told him he could tell me where my husband's body was or I could hold a press conference this afternoon. Now, am I going to have problems with you?"

Rodriguez glared at me as if it were all my fault and stepped aside. Marie walked down the gangway and straight into room 235. Kelli Spencer looked like she'd been waiting for her. Spencer took Marie's hands in hers, and the two women walked over to the bed. Spencer whispered a few words. Marie took her time, leaning in for a last look at her husband. When she was satisfied, she nodded at Spencer, who wasn't laughing with her eyes anymore.

"That's my husband."

The three of us stood in the parking lot of the Ambassador Motel. Marie had herself a smoke. The morning sun was harsh on her face, and I thought she didn't look much different from her husband lying upstairs.

"What happened to your hand, Mr. Kelly?"

"I cut my finger. I'm sorry about Ray."

Her eyes flashed, then went flat again. "I told you he was dead."

"How did you know?"

"I didn't know. It was just a feeling."

"We suspect Ray died from natural causes," Rodriguez said. "Maybe cancer."

She responded with a flick of her shoulders. "The coroner explained it all."

"Was your husband in good health when you last saw him?" Rodriguez said.

"That was more than two years ago, Detective, but yes, Ray was in perfect health." She pointed the burning end of her cigarette at the cinder-block building. "How did he wind up here?"

"Good question, ma'am. Except for his clothes, we found no personal belongings in the room, and the desk downstairs says he never checked in."

"I don't understand."

"Someone broke into the room, probably last night, and left the body. Then they tipped the police to its whereabouts."

"That's difficult to believe."

"The coroner also thinks he's been dead awhile. His body temperature indicates he might have been stored in a refrigerated space somewhere." Rodriguez watched Marie closely, daring her to fill in the blanks. Her gaze shifted from Rodriguez to me and back again.

"Are you expecting me to provide some explanation, Detective?"

"Ray died of natural causes, Ms. Perry, but he wasn't alone. Someone clearly moved the body and they must have had a good reason."

"Sorry I can't be of more help. Am I free to go?"

"What's the best way to reach you if we have some follow-up questions?"

"I have an appointment tomorrow morning. Otherwise, I should be available on my cell. I assume you have the number?"

Rodriguez nodded.

She dropped her cigarette to the ground and crushed it with a twist of her toe. "By the way, the media . . ."

"So far, it's been quiet. At some point, the coroner will make a statement saying they found Ray. After that . . ." Rodriguez shrugged.

"How long?"

"A couple of days. Maybe a week."

"Will they call me before they release the report?"

"Of course."

"Thank you, Detective."

We watched her walk across the lot to her car. She gave me a final look before ducking inside. Then she was gone.

"What do you think?" I said.

"If Ray hadn't died of natural causes, I'd be taking her in for questioning."

"That bad, huh?"

"Count on it." Rodriguez pulled out a long yellow envelope and handed it to me.

"What's this?" I said.

"Your boy, Rafael Ramirez."

"What about him?"

"He's working tonight. Gets off at midnight. I'll pick you up."

"Why?"

"Read the report. I'll see you tonight. And if I were you, I'd keep an eye on the widow Perry."

CHAPTER 31

Rafael Ramirez worked out of the Twelfth District on the city's Near West Side. Rodriguez and I sat in the police parking lot twenty yards from his car, a late-model Jeep Cherokee.

"What time does he get off?" I said.

Rodriguez checked his watch. "Another couple of minutes."

"I can do this on my own, Vince."

Rodriguez flicked a finger, one of ten he had wrapped around the steering wheel. "I want him to know."

We sat for another minute. A car buzzed down Racine Avenue, a girl hanging out the window yelling something I couldn't make out. Then it was quiet again.

"What happened with Ray?" I said.

"They got back some preliminary blood work. Definitely leukemia. Doc says he'd probably been sick less than a year."

"Makes no sense."

"And yet there it is. Coroner says they can sit on the report for a week, tops."

A rectangle of light appeared as a door opened. A couple of off-duty cops, a man and a woman, came out and wandered toward their cars. Then, a couple more.

"What are you gonna do with her?" Rodriguez said. He didn't have to tell me who he was talking about.

"Well, we know she didn't kill Ray."

"She knows who put him in the Ambassador. I can guarantee you that."

The door opened again, and Ramirez came out alone. He was short, maybe five seven, and thick with quick-twitch muscle. Rodriguez told me he'd been a boxer and liked to show off with his fists. Part of me looked forward to that; the rest of me knew it probably wouldn't go that way. Rodriguez got out of the car first.

"Ramirez?"

Rodriguez cut off the smaller man's path to his vehicle. I moved in behind so he couldn't see the cop shop either. Ramirez shot a quick look my way, then jutted his chin out at Rodriguez.

"That's right. Who are you?"

The detective flashed his star. "Rodriguez. Violent Crimes."

"I don't know you."

"Yeah. Listen, you got a minute to talk?"

"Who's your pal?" Ramirez jerked his head toward me without actually looking me in the eye.

"He's a PI. Working with me on a case."

"What do you want?"

Rodriguez glanced around the empty lot. "Might be easier if we went somewhere. Maybe a cup of coffee?"

"I just finished a ten-hour shift. Nothing I want except a couple of cold beers, some dinner, and bed."

"I understand," Rodriguez said. "This won't take a minute."

Ramirez shook his head and sighed.

"You'd really be helping us out," Rodriguez said.

Ramirez pulled out a key fob and unlocked the doors to his jeep. "Follow me."

We went to a cop bar on Ogden called JoJo's. The only thing marking the bar's existence was an Old Style sign hung crooked in the window. Ramirez pressed a white button by the front door. Ten seconds later, a buzzer sounded, and we were in. The layout was basic. A long wooden counter, a few booths and some high-top tables, a single TV up in the corner. One wall was full of police patches from around the world. To the left of the front door was a jukebox and a glassed-in display with the names and faces of officers killed in the line of duty. The midnight shift had filled the place, maybe a dozen drinkers on stools and another dozen working away at the tables and booths. Most of the cops were drinking beer and whiskey. Some were drinking whiskey and beer. The bartender was pulling red-and-white cans of Budweiser out of a blue cooler filled with ice and telling anyone who'd listen he'd just made some ham-and-cheese sandwiches. I ordered us three beers and a shot of Jack for Ramirez. We got our drinks and found a booth in a far corner of the place. Ramirez knocked back the Jack first thing. Then he popped open the Bud, took a sip, and belched. "What is it you want to talk about?"

I waited on Rodriguez, who pulled out a manila envelope and put it on the table.

"What the fuck is that?" Ramirez said. He still had his gun strapped to his belt; his forehead and scalp popped with sweat.

"Relax," Rodriguez said. I took a quick look around. No one had said a word to us coming in, but I figured the place had to be full of Ramirez's buddies. If Ramirez had any buddies. Rodriguez opened up the envelope and took out a small DV tape.

"I'm gonna show you this, Ramirez, but only if you want to see it. If you don't, it goes back in the envelope. All right?"

"I don't have time for this bullshit," Ramirez said, but didn't go anywhere. I noticed he never took his eyes off the tape.

"I've got a friend," Rodriguez said. "His name's Eddie Mahoney. You know him?"

Ramirez shook his head.

"Eddie's got seven kids, six of 'em girls. Goes to mass every Sunday and works Vice the rest of the week. Weird, right? But that's Eddie. Anyway, he ran a sting about a year and a half ago. Targeted underage girls on a couple of the West Side strolls." Rodriguez's voice softened a touch. He tickled the DV tape with a finger. "She was small and dark. Told you her name was Luisa. Eddie shot the video from a van across the street. The two of you in an unmarked squad car."

Ramirez gripped and regripped his beer can, creasing the aluminum with his fingers.

"You hear me, Ramirez?"

"I heard you. What do you want?"

"The girl was fifteen. Eddie gave you a pass because you were a cop. He wasn't so happy when I told him how you treated your oldest daughter." Rodriguez took out a copy of the police report Elena Ramirez had given me and pushed it across the table. "When was the last time you saw Lourdes?"

Ramirez glanced at the report and pushed it back.

"Doesn't matter," Rodriguez said. "It's your other daughters we're concerned about. We think they need a dad. Not some asshole pointing a gun at them."

I watched the vein pulse in his neck, but Ramirez didn't say a word.

"We own you," Rodriguez said, flicking a finger between himself and me. "We don't want to own you, but we do. So go home and start being a man. Take care of your wife. Take care of the three girls you have left. And consider yourself lucky. Think you can do that?"

Ramirez stared at his boots, then the barroom floor and nodded.

"Good. Do it, and the tape gets buried. Fuck with anyone in your family, and I'll make sure you pull at least twenty-five for statutory rape. And I'll make sure it hurts. Now get out of here."

We watched Ramirez leave. "Asshole," Rodriguez muttered. We both ordered shots of Jack, finished our beers, and followed him out the door. It was late. And I had an early start in the morning.

CHAPTER 32

The clock on my dashboard read 7:15 a.m. I was camped out on Marie Perry's block with a thermos of coffee and a stack of ham-and-cheese sandwiches I'd bought from the bartender at JoJo's. I was halfway through my second when the lights in her kitchen flicked on. The door to an attached garage opened at exactly eight-thirty, and Marie's Lexus wheeled away. I waited another fifteen minutes, then walked up to the brownstone and pressed the buzzer for the third floor. A woman's voice rang down over the intercom. I told her I had a package and needed to leave it in the lobby. There was a small pause before she buzzed me in. I placed an empty FedEx box with no address on a chair by the mailboxes and walked upstairs. Marie Perry's apartment was the only one on the first floor. I crouched down by the front door, pulled out the red leather case I'd brought with me, and unzipped it. The lock picks were made of stainless steel and laid out in a row on a soft velvet pad. In a sleeve behind the picks were two silver "bump" keys. Each was cut almost flat, with tiny teeth of identical height. The first key didn't fit into the lock, so I tried the second. It slid in smoothly. I pulled the key out a fraction, turned it as far as it would go to the right, and held it. Then I took out a small yellow hammer and tapped the key all the way back into the lock. The key "bumped" past the last pin in the lock, causing the entire pin stack to jump at once and clear the cylinder. The key turned the rest of the way, and the door to Marie Perry's apartment opened. It had taken all of a minute and a half.

I closed the door behind me and made a quick and quiet tour of the place. Once I was sure I was alone, I found my way into the back room where Marie had stashed Ray Perry's old desk. I looked through all the drawers starting at the bottom. Not a scrap of interesting paper in any of them. Behind the desk were some file cabinets. I pulled them open and came up empty again. I sat behind Ray's desk. To the right of the blotter were two pens and a letter opener. Arrayed on the other side were three framed pictures. One was a wedding day photo of Ray and Marie. One was Ray Perry being sworn in as governor. The third was a small black-and-white snapshot of Ray in what looked like a hospital room. His face was cast in profile, and he was cradling an infant close to his chest. I picked up the picture and studied it. There was something odd there, but I couldn't place it. I put the picture down and went back through the apartment to the kitchen. I was wondering if I had enough time to give the entire place a toss when I saw a hook on the wall next to the refrigerator. It had a set of keys on it with a tag that read RAY'S CADDY. I grabbed the keys and went down a run of stairs to the garage.

The Caddy was sitting beside the empty slot for Marie's Lexus. I opened the door and slid behind the wheel. The car was loaded, full leather, power everything, and a complete navigation system. I turned over the engine and hit a button on the nav menu that read PRIOR TRIPS. Up came a list of addresses and dates. The latest trip registered was two years ago—a week before Ray Perry was sentenced to prison. He'd accessed directions to two addresses: 741 West Hickory Street in the western suburb of Hinsdale and 23 Cabot Street in the adjoining suburb of Clarendon Hills. I jotted down both addresses and gave the rest of the car a quick once-over. The interior was spotless. Just for kicks, I popped the trunk. Empty. I pulled up the trunk liner, expecting to find the spare tire tucked somewhere underneath. Instead I found a black metal box with a lock, sunk into what used to be the tire well. The lock hadn't been disturbed, which told me either the feds had missed the box altogether or they'd found the key to it. Knowing the feds, I was guessing the former. I took out my hammer and used a flat chisel to pop the box open. Inside was a stack of file folders. The first few contained Ray Perry's birth certificate and school diplomas, the Perrys' marriage certificate, and what appeared to be a will. Underneath that were a couple of medical reports summarizing Ray's annual physicals. At the very bottom I found a handful of older files, torn and creased with age. One had HIGH SCHOOL scrawled in black pen across the front. Another was baby blue and had a picture of Ray holding an infant clipped to the cover. It was the same photo I'd seen on Ray's desk and stirred up the same queasy feeling. I put the file aside and was about to dig into the rest when I heard a soft thump upstairs. I'd left the kitchen door open. Now I crept up the stairs and listened. There was movement in the front of the apartment. Heels on wood. Light, quick footsteps. I closed the kitchen door and went back down to the garage. I stuffed the files from the strong box into a small duffel bag I'd brought with me and put the box back into the tire well. Then I closed the trunk and left the Caddy's keys on a window ledge. There was a single door in the garage that led directly to an alley. I slipped out, walked down the alley, and found my car. Marie's Lexus was parked at the curb with its blinkers on. Five minutes later she came out with a black satchel in her left hand. I waited until she'd gotten in her car and turned the corner. Then I followed.

She stopped to get coffee and drop off some dry cleaning. During the stops, I knocked back a couple of Tylenol for the hand and took another call from Northwestern wondering why I'd left their hospital without checking out. At eleven-fifteen, Marie pulled into the parking lot of North Community Bank on the 3600 block of North Broadway. If things were going to get interesting, this was as good a place as any. She took the satchel out of the backseat of her car and walked into the bank. I watched through the plate-glass windows as she floated past a row of tellers to a heavyset woman sitting in an open cubicle. Marie sat down, and the two women talked for a minute or two. Then they both got up and disappeared down a set of stairs. I jumped out of the car and walked across the street.

North Community was a pet-friendly bank. I knew that because of the sign, as well as the chocolate Lab puppy who slipped his leash and flew at me as I came through the door. I snagged the pup by the collar and engaged in the requisite oohing and aahing with the owner and one of the tellers. I hadn't wanted to attract attention to myself, but the Lab actually helped. Once he was back on leash, the owner returned to her banking, and everyone else in the place seemed to forget about me. I walked by the cubicle Marie had stopped at and picked up a business card from a stack on the desk. The card read:

COLLEEN BRASHLER
PERSONAL BANKING

I put the card in my pocket and continued toward the dark set of stairs Marie and Colleen had just descended. A sign on the wall read VAULTS AND SAFE-DEPOSIT BOXES, with an arrow pointing down. I heard a door open below and, with a quick scratch behind the ears for the Lab, made my way back through the bank. I'd just climbed behind the wheel when Marie Perry walked out. She carried the leather satchel in her right hand. It might have been my imagination, but it looked a good deal fatter than when she went in.

I followed Marie's car down Broadway and then east on Belmont. I wasn't much for playing the lottery. As we drove, however, I felt like I was holding a ticket and waiting for the Ping-Pong balls to drop. First, we jumped on Lake Shore Drive heading south. Then we picked up the Ike with a full load of traffic streaming west. Finally, we turned onto Route 83 and snaked south toward the villages of Hinsdale and Clarendon Hills. I took out my notebook and checked the two addresses I'd pulled from Ray Perry's Caddy. I figured I had a winner. We got off the highway in Clarendon Hills and cruised past a golf course before taking a left on Norfolk Avenue. Up ahead I saw a sign for Cabot Street. Marie hit her blinker. I went around the block and came up Cabot from the other side. Number 23 was one of a half-dozen cookie-cutter Colonials sprinkled up and down the street. This one had white shutters and a mailbox out front that read MCBAIN. Marie Perry's Lexus was parked in the driveway.

I got out of the car, zipped up my jacket, and took a walk past the house. The shades were open, and I could see two women sitting together on a couch in the living room. Their heads were close together. The satchel was on the table in front of them. I crossed the street and walked back to my car. A quick web search for the address on my phone produced nothing of interest. Then I opened up my laptop and searched for MCBAIN on my hard drive. The first thing that popped up was some notes I'd made from my conversation with Jack O'Donnell. He'd flagged at least three fatal car crashes as having been caused by Beacon's faulty highway construction.

One of them was in May of 2010. A father and three kids were killed when their vehicle flipped on the Eisenhower. The dad's name was Frank McBain. The only survivor of the crash was his wife, Melissa.

I pulled up a half-dozen articles on the crash. A photo from the *Trib* showed three neighbors standing in front of the house I was looking at, arms around one another, sobbing into their sleeves. I was reading the article when Marie Perry stepped out of the house. Melissa McBain stayed inside, the screen door shut between them. The two women continued to talk for another four or five minutes. Then Marie walked back down the driveway to her car. She had the black bag with her.

I watched Marie drive down Cabot Street and disappear. Melissa McBain stood by the windows in her living room and watched as well. Then she tugged the curtains shut. I took my time leaving the neighborhood. After all, Hinsdale was only a mile away, and I already knew exactly where Marie Perry was headed.

CHAPTER 33

On January 6, 2011, Rick Beckerman went out to pick up a pizza and some beer. Beckerman was a sixty-eight-year-old cardiologist who had decided to hang up his stethoscope and move to Santa Fe. He and his wife, Julie, had just accepted an offer on their Hinsdale home that afternoon and set a closing date. The Beckermans were planning to toast the house they raised their three kids in, then look at pictures of the place they were building in the desert. Moving on. Moving out. Beckerman jumped on the Ike for the six-mile drive back from Pino's Pizza. He'd gone about a mile and a half when his left front tire hit a crack in the blacktop and split wide open. Beckerman's BMW was on its side in the time it took to change the radio station. The last thing he felt was hot asphalt crushing one side of his face. The last thing he saw was the cold steel of the guardrail.

I sat on West Hickory Street in Hinsdale and stared at number 741. Julie Beckerman had never made it to Santa Fe. After her husband was killed, she decided to keep the house and live with her ghosts. A lot of people played out their lives that way, wrapping themselves up in their pain and dying a little bit every day.

I got out of my car and walked down Hickory. Marie's Lexus was parked in front of the Beckerman house; all the shades were pulled tight. No matter. I knew she was in there with her black bag. Doing what was another story.

She came out an hour later. I tried to get a look at Julie Beckerman, but all I got was the flash of a white head before the door swung shut. Marie jumped in her car and started driving again. I didn't let her get too far ahead this time. I was out of addresses and had no idea where she might be going next.

We drove a half mile and stopped at a quick mart. Marie went in and came out with a sack full of groceries. We jumped back on the highway and drove south into neighboring Willowbrook. Marie got off at Sixty-Seventh Street and turned down a small street called Old Harbor Road. She left the satchel in the car this time and took the groceries instead. I watched as she walked up to house number 254 and hit the doorbell. The door was opened by a teenaged girl with reddish hair. Behind her was another girl, younger with blond hair. I snapped a picture as Marie stepped inside and jotted down the address in my book. Then I plugged the address into Google, but couldn't find out who lived there. I rechecked my notes on the accidents O'Donnell had given me. There was nothing with a Willowbrook address, but that didn't mean someone hadn't moved. I thought about the satchel. And the groceries. Maybe Willowbrook was different. I idly considered breaking into the Lexus and seeing what was in the black bag, but I had a hunch I already knew. Marie was funneling cash to victims of the Beacon accidents. The question was why. And on behalf of whom. I hit a couple of buttons on my CD player and Springsteen's *Nebraska* filled the car. I leaned back in my seat and stared at the front door to 254 Old Harbor Road. And waited.

CHAPTER 34

The professional sat a half block away and ran through a menu of possible weapons. A rifle with a scope. A heavy-caliber handgun for stopping power. The .22 with its customized pearl-handle grip. A smartphone buzzed on the dashboard of the car. It was a text confirming the job. The professional trashed the text and studied the target. Kelly was slumped in the front seat, staring down the street, waiting for Marie Perry. The professional didn't know why the house mattered to Kelly and didn't much give a damn. He'd been warned off, but it didn't take. And so it went. The money had been deposited in the account. The job was a go.

The professional began to build an image of the kill. Details shifted and locked into place. Contingencies and angles. Movement, action. The job seemed like an easy one. The professional knew, however, not to trust that too hard. Marie Perry appeared on the steps outside the house and began to walk toward her car. The professional took the .22 out of the glove compartment. Kelly was up in his seat, engine running.

CHAPTER 35

I listened to *Nebraska* in its entirety before the door to 254 Old Harbor swung open again. Marie walked down a short run of steps, fumbled for a moment with her keys, and turned to scan the street. Her eyes flicked over my car, but I was too far back for her to see anything but a dark lump. I'd just slipped the engine into gear when I caught a flash of something in my rearview mirror. I turned to look as a man came up on the passenger's side and knocked on the window. His ring made a heavy, dead sound on the glass. I lowered the window and leaned over.

"Excuse me," the man said and reached under his coat. My fingers brushed the grip on my gun as he pulled out a small blue notebook. "My wife noticed you've been sitting out here for a while. May I ask what you're doing?"

I fished out a card with a name on it that wasn't mine. "I'm a private investigator. Former cop."

The man put on a pair of reading glasses and studied the card. Then he copied down some information in his notebook. "A cop, huh? Why would a cop be in this neighborhood?" He smiled in that faux-friendly, suburban sort of way. "You wouldn't happen to have some sort of identification?"

Up ahead, Marie was pulling away from the curb.

"I do have an ID," I said. "It's in my hip pocket, right beside my gun." I gestured to the piece and watched his eyes widen. "Unfortunately, I'm not gonna have time to show it to you. You see that Lexus?" I pointed at Marie's car, about to turn the corner at the end of the block. "I've got maybe thirty seconds to get on her tail or I lose her altogether. Okay?"

"Well . . ." The man frowned down his nose and looked like he wanted to call a meeting. He seemed like a meeting kind of guy. I, on the other hand, was not.

"Tell your wife I'm sorry, pal. Gotta run." I raised the window and hit the gas, glancing at my friend in the rearview mirror and wondering if I'd get out of Willowbrook before he called the cops. Fifteen minutes later, I was safely back on the highway, tailing the Lexus east, down the throat of the Ike and back into the city.

As we hit the Loop, I eased back and gave the Lexus some room. We cruised past the arched windows and watchful owls atop the Harold Washington Library before cutting across Grant Park and up onto Lake Shore Drive. The Lexus exited the drive at Belmont and took a left on Southport Avenue. I watched from a half block away as Marie parked the car and walked down the street, black bag in hand. Then I got out and followed. She ducked into the front door of Saint Alphonsus just as I hit the corner at Lincoln. I grabbed a cup of coffee at a diner called the Golden Apple and found a window seat with a good view of the church. Ten minutes slipped by. I finished my coffee, walked across the street, and went inside.

The stone floor felt rough under my feet; the smell of melted wax and incense hung in the air. I touched my fingers to the holy water and let my eyes adjust to the darkness. To my right was a small wooden door with a Celtic cross carved into it. I opened it and crept up a flight of stairs to a loft that held the church's freestanding organ. I sat on a bench reserved for the choir and looked down.

Soft light filtered through stained-glass windows, throwing painted shadows across row after row of empty pews. An Asian woman knelt in the very front, staring at a crucified Christ hanging behind the altar. In a side nave, an elderly couple sat together before a couple of confessional boxes. A red light burned above one of them. I had a pretty good idea who was inside.

Five minutes later, the light clicked off, and the door to the box opened. Marie came out and went straight to a pew where she knelt and bent her head to pray some more. Eventually, the elderly couple left. Then the Asian woman. A priest came out of the confessional wearing a long black cassock trimmed in red. He walked up to an altar lit by a single candle, genuflected, and disappeared into the sacristy. After that, it was just me and Marie. Her praying. Me watching. A side door scraped open to Marie's left, and two men came in wearing cloth coats and dark caps. One took off his cap and poked the other to do the same. The men looked awkward, out of place. They trudged up and down the aisles, scanning pews and ignoring Marie, who sat on the bench and stared straight ahead. When they were done, the two men disappeared underneath my perch. Neither of them ever bothered to look up.

The candle on the altar danced and flickered in an invisible breeze before expiring in a gray thread of smoke. On cue, the side door scraped open again, and Bones McIntyre walked in. He kept his hands in his pockets and made his way straight for Marie. The two talked for twenty-five minutes. Bones appeared to be doing the heavy lifting. Marie mostly shook her head yes or no. Father and daughter never touched the entire time they were together.

Bones went out the same door he came in, Marie's black satchel tucked under his arm. Ten minutes after he left, she followed. I stayed long enough to mumble a handful of Hail Marys and an equally rusty Our Father. Then I left, too. And the church never batted an eye.

The professional studied Kelly in the rearview mirror as he exited the church. The detective's hands were slouched in his pockets, and his head was down, but Kelly's eyes were alive. He walked across the intersection with a fluid grace; the gun sat easy on his hip. The kill would have to be quick. And Kelly couldn't see it coming. The professional thought about the pearl-handled .22, sitting once again in the glove compartment. It was perfect for the job. Everything else was just a matter of time and circumstance. Kelly climbed into his car and swung into the stream of early evening traffic. The professional let a bus go past, then tucked in behind it and followed.

CHAPTER 36

I parked my car on Addison and walked down Lakewood Avenue toward my apartment. I thought about what I'd seen inside the church and tried to fit it into a larger picture. I was tired, however, and my hand ached. Not to mention my head. I wanted nothing more than a glass of whiskey, a couple of Tylenol, and an early night in bed.

I was crossing Eddy Street when I felt a car come up behind me and slow. My neck began to tingle, and my fingers started to twitch. I drifted toward the cover of an open doorway and reached into my duffel bag. It was still full of the paperwork I'd taken from the trunk of Ray Perry's car. Underneath that was a .40-caliber Glock. I took out the gun and kept it at my side as I turned. The car was a late-model Honda. The woman behind the wheel beeped her horn once and waved. I slid the gun back into my bag and raised my bandaged hand. Karen Simone got out and walked over.

"What happened to you?" she said, touching her own hand and wincing.

"I cut myself. What are you doing here?"

"I live on Racine, just south of Belmont." She gestured back to the Honda, parked in front of a hydrant with its blinkers flashing. "I stopped at the Jewel for a few things. That's a hell of a bandage, Michael. How did you do it?"

"Long story."

"Were you working on Ray's case?"

"Another time, Karen. Right now, all I want to do is get some dinner and go to bed."

"Okay, I'll let you go."

"Sorry."

"Don't worry about it." She leaned in and gave me a quick kiss on the cheek. "Take care of yourself."

"Thanks. I'll see you." I turned toward my building and took out my keys. I'd just gotten the front door open when Karen pulled up and rolled down her window.

"Hey."

"Hey."

"I just bought the fixings for chicken parmigiana. Thing is, I always make too much."

"And?"

"Jeez, do I have to send up smoke signals? Come over and eat. I'll do all the work, and you can lie on the couch like a bum."

My first thought was no. Then I reviewed the current contents of my refrigerator—to wit, four slices of wrapped cheese and three kinds of mustard. I also had beer and a loaf of stale bread.

"I have to feed my dog."

"I can wait."

"Do you have whiskey?"

She frowned. "I have wine."

"Good. I'll bring the whiskey."

I let Karen into my building just as another car swept past.

The driver, a man with coarse stubble covering his cheeks and jaw, stared at us intently. I felt the tingle again at the back of my scalp and watched the car until it disappeared down the block.

Karen lived in an old warehouse that had been converted into lofts. The floor plan was open with a kitchen and living room on the first floor and a single bedroom up a short flight of stairs. As promised, Karen sat me on a soft couch with a TV and a glass of Oban single malt. Pretty soon the apartment was filling up with the nut smell of melted butter mingled with garlic. I got up off the couch and took a seat at a long granite counter that looked into the kitchen. Karen had pulled her hair back and put on an apron.

"Smells great," I said.

"Garlic, onions, and butter. Hard to go wrong." She chopped up some olives and added them to the pan, then stirred the whole thing with a wooden spoon.

"You need some help?" I said.

She pointed to the refrigerator. "You could get the chicken out."

I pulled out a couple of boneless chicken breasts. Karen got me a small wooden mallet and showed me how to pound the chicken flat.

"I didn't know you could cook with a hammer."

"Go to it."

I beat the bird into submission . . . or at least into cutlets. Karen opened a can of crushed tomatoes and dumped them into the pan. Red sauce spattered her arms, neck, and cheeks.

"Oops," she said, and we both laughed. I found a towel and watched as she wiped off the sauce.

"Glad you came over?" she said.

"It's kind of fun."

Karen seasoned the sauce and stirred.

"How long have you had this place?" I said.

"I got it as a sublease once everything went crazy with the stories about me and Ray. I can get out with a month's notice."

Like her office, the apartment was sparsely appointed and devoid of any personal touches. Karen Simone didn't allow a lot of baggage in her life. I remembered when I used to be that way.

"You've got a pretty good gash over your eyebrow," she said and pointed with her spoon.

"I was thinking it adds character."

"Really?"

"You don't think so?"

"I guess it goes with the hand. Just try not to bleed on anything. Now, go and watch TV. We'll eat in a half hour, give or take."

I went back to the couch and poured another finger of Oban, savoring the traces of woodsmoke and peat. On ESPN, they were running highlights of the Cubs figuring out new ways to lose baseball games. I watched for a few minutes, then wandered back to the kitchen.

"You come out here, I'm gonna put you to work."

"I'm all yours."

"Pull out the black pot for pasta. It's in the top cabinet."

I filled the pot with water, salted it, and set it to boil. Karen dredged the cutlets in flour, egg, and bread crumbs, then began to brown them in a skillet. I tasted the sauce.

"How is it?" She turned one of the cutlets over and adjusted the heat under the pan.

"Perfect."

Karen pointed to a baking dish she'd put out on the counter. "Do me a favor and cover the bottom of that with a layer of sauce." I did as I was told. Karen transferred the cutlets from pan to dish, ladled another layer of sauce over them, then topped the whole thing with slices of mozzarella, fresh basil, and a dusting of Parmesan cheese. Finally, she popped the dish in the oven.

"Fifteen minutes and it's done."

"Looks pretty good."

"Thanks. You want to grab some plates and silverware." She nodded to a set of drawers. "And pick out some wine for dinner. There should be a couple of bottles in the cabinet."

I found the silverware and opened a bottle of red. Karen dumped a fistful of pasta into the pot of boiling water and stirred. Ten minutes later, a timer went off. Karen took out the chicken and put it up on the stove top. The pasta was drained, and a green salad appeared from nowhere. She made a few final adjustments, and dinner was ready.

We ate at the counter. The chicken parm was perfect; the sauce, amazing. Or maybe I just hadn't eaten a decent meal in a week and a half. Either way, I dug in. Karen picked at her food and sipped her wine.

"Sorry," I said. "Guess I'm hungrier than I thought."

"Please. You compliment the chef."

"Where did you learn to cook like this?"

"TV. Books. It's not hard. And it takes my mind off things."

"What kind of things?"

"You know. Nothing. Everything."

I could see the strain in her eyes and wondered what it meant.

"Does it hurt?" she said and touched the back of my hand.

"It looks worse than it is."

"It looks pretty bad." She cut off a small piece of chicken and chewed. "Are you going to tell me what happened?"

"No."

"Are you going to update me on Ray?"

"No." I tore off a piece of French bread and used it to soak up some red sauce. The room went quiet, save for the rub of plates and silverware.

"You asked me to keep an eye out for anyone coming into the charity claiming to be from a company called Beacon."

I felt my head snap up. "And?"

"Are they still part of your case?"

"This isn't a game, Karen. Did someone come in?"

"Was it Beacon who hurt you?"

I put down my knife and fork and leaned across the counter. "Who came in?"

"No one. Not a soul."

I studied her for a moment, then leaned back. "Good."

"You're really worried?"

"It's dangerous. And I don't want you to get hurt."

"I'd prefer neither of us gets hurt."

"Me, too."

"You won't let me help?"

I shook my head.

"And you won't let it go?"

"I wish it was that easy."

She reached out and touched my cheek. I felt the distance in her fingertips, the callus of someone who understands the business of being alone. Even if she doesn't like it. "Are you done?"

I nodded and helped her clean up. When we were finished, she took my arms and wrapped them around her waist. "I just want you to be safe, Michael. That's all."

"I'll do my best."

"I know you will." She leaned in to kiss me. Long and slow and full. Then she took me by the hand and led me upstairs.

CHAPTER 37

The bed was wide; the sheets fresh and cool. I watched as she unbuttoned my shirt. She took it off carefully, slipping it over the thick bandage.

"Does it hurt?" she whispered. I shook my head. She unwrapped the outer dressing, then the white pad underneath. I sat on the edge of the bed as she peeled off the final layer of gauze. She turned the hand gently and winced when she saw the run of stitches.

"I told you," I said. "It looks worse than it is."

She kissed my wrist, open palm, then each of my fingers. I lay back in bed. She brought in a pitcher of warm water and washed my hand. Then she found some fresh gauze and rewrapped it. I tried to speak, but she touched my lips with her finger and slipped away again. In the darkness, I heard a whisper of cotton, the rustle of silk. Then she was back, strong hands running down my chest and across my stomach, tugging at whatever clothes remained between us. She kissed me lightly at first, tracing the wounds on my face, licking the skin dry. I watched as she slid up on top of me and leaned back in a column of blue light. She kept her eyes closed and began to work up and down, moving in slow circles, gripping first my shoulders, then leaning forward and bracing herself against the headboard. I matched her rhythm and felt myself fill her. She made a stirring sound in her throat. Neither of us made another until the end when she raked my skin with her nails and cried out softly. Then she was back beside me, breath tickling my cheek, heart drumming against my chest. I kissed the curve of her neck. She put two fingers to my lips and rolled over so her back was to me. Then she took my bandaged hand and drew it across her stomach. And that's how we fell asleep.

CHAPTER 38

There was movement somewhere in the apartment. I rolled over and felt for Karen. The bed was empty. The sheets, rumpled and warm. It was still night, and I looked down the short flight of stairs toward the living room, lined with bars of light from the street. She was standing by the windows, wrapped loosely in a robe. Shadows played across her face from the moving traffic below.

"Hey," I said.

Karen started as if waking from a dream, then looked up and smiled. Slow and lazy. "Did I wake you?"

"I thought I heard something." I began to get out of bed.

"Stay. I'm coming up." She cinched the robe around her waist and walked softly toward the stairs. I watched her bend down in one motion and pick up a flat black purse sitting on a table. She kept both hands on the purse as she moved, more quickly now, across the room. The purse struck me as odd. The way she was carrying it, even stranger. As she hit the first step, her right hand slipped inside the purse. I caught a glimpse of a gleaming white handle and dove for a couple of feet of floor between the wall and the bed. The first bullet burst the pillow my head had been lying on. The second buried itself in the wall above me. I hugged the rough weave of carpet. Karen kicked some blankets out of the way and moved deliberately around the bed. Then she was over me, the lower half of her face gouged by shadow, her eyes the color of machinery. Whoever Karen Simone was, she'd done this before and wouldn't waste another bullet.

A hundred million thoughts buzzed through my brain, all pleading for attention, all demanding a reprieve. She laid the gun on my forehead and paused for half a breath. As it turned out, her final breath. The suppressed round knocked her neatly against the wall. Karen Simone landed faceup on the bed, a small hole drilled halfway between her temple and her ear. Ten feet away, a man with a rifle came up the short run of stairs. He was silhouetted by light from the living room and moved quickly to check for a pulse. Then Andrew Wallace crouched beside me and put a finger to his lips.

"She was going to kill you, Michael." Wallace grabbed the black purse and threw it at me. Inside was a customized sleeve for the gun, as well as four different driver's licenses and three passports. All of them had Karen's picture and different names.

"Beacon put her into Ray's office to get close to him. She was supposed to keep an eye on him during the trial, kill him if she thought he was going to cut a deal with the feds. When Ray disappeared with their money, they kept her in place hoping something would turn up."

I looked at Karen, mouth open slightly, eyes already starting to cloud. Her right hand trailed off the bed. The .22-caliber pistol with the pearl-handle grip lay on the rug a few feet away. My thoughts wandered back to our night at Sterch's—the smoke, her laughter, the beer. I thought about an e-mail

I'd told her about, from a former transportation writer for the *Trib*. A guy who wanted to meet with me. A guy who was helping me on a case. With that mention, I'd effectively signed Jack O'Donnell's death warrant. And I was probably looking at his killer.

"We've got to move," Wallace said. The erstwhile grad student turned ninja had camo black smeared down his cheeks and across his forehead.

"Why should I trust you?" I said.

"Because I'm the guy who's gonna get us out of here. There are three more shooters outside. They were supposed to kill Karen after she called in that she'd finished you." Wallace pulled a .40-caliber handgun out of his vest and nodded at the bandage on my hand. "Can you shoot?"

I took the gun and began to get dressed. Wallace kept an eye on the street from the living room. We went through the kitchen and crawled out a back door that led to a deck, a flight of stairs, and an alley. There was a car parked under a streetlight at the end of the alley. I peeked over the deck railing and saw two heads in the front seat.

"There's two back here and one out front," Wallace said. "Good news is they're not nearly as dangerous as Karen."

"Bad news is there's three of them."

"I'll take out the driver. When I do, you head down the stairs. See if you can tag his buddy. I'll go back through the apartment and get the guy out front. Okay?"

I nodded and crouched on the landing. Wallace laid the barrel of his rifle over the railing. He put his eye to the scope, paused a moment, then squeezed off a round. I was halfway down the stairs as the windshield exploded, ten yards away when the passenger's door popped open. I put two rounds through it. A body rolled out onto the pavement. I put another round in him, waited a beat, then moved closer. The guy I'd put down was dead. The inside of the car, a spray of blood and tissue. I picked up a gun that had bounced out of the car and put it in my pocket. A second windshield shattering told me Wallace had hit the third shooter. I ran toward the front of the building as Wallace came around a corner.

"Come on."

We ran back the way I'd come, past the alley and down a couple of side streets. Wallace had a dark blue sedan tucked underneath a viaduct. Five minutes later, we were driving west on Diversey Avenue. Wallace wiped the black off his face and tossed his rifle under a tarp in the backseat. I still had the .40-cal.

"You probably have a lot of questions," Wallace said.

"A few."

"I'll try to answer as many as I can, but you need to trust me."

"We'll see."

Wallace pulled up to a light at Damen Avenue. The clock in front of a bank read 3:43. The intersection was empty. I could hear the first wail of sirens behind us.

"Do me a favor and toss the gun in the backseat," Wallace said.

"There's a twenty-four-hour pancake house called the Golden Nugget at Diversey and Western. Pull into the lot."

"I don't feel like pancakes, Michael. And those places are full of cops."

I lifted the gun an inch. "Just pull in."

I had Wallace drive to the very back of the lot and turn off the engine. A trucker came out of the restaurant with a toothpick wedged in his mouth. He started up his rig and rumbled into the night.

"I know about Beacon," I said. "And I know about the money Ray took."

"Then you know they want it back."

"You worked for Ray?"

"For a long time."

"What about Marie?"

"She didn't know about me until recently. But she did help Ray escape. I was impressed as hell you put that together, by the way. I never would have given you those courthouse pictures if I knew what you were going to do with them."

"Did you actually take them?"

"At Ray's request. He thought they might come in handy someday."

"Did Marie know about the money?"

Wallace shook his head. "At first, no."

"And now?"

"Now she knows."

"How was Ray able to rip off Beacon?"

"I set it up."

"Talented guy. Why didn't you and Ray just grab the cash and never look back?"

"Not as easy as it sounds. Besides, Marie was still here. She didn't want to breathe the same air as him, but Ray loved her anyway. He wanted to make sure she was safe. Especially once he got sick."

"Why hire me?"

"I told you. Ray knew Beacon would plant people close to him once he was indicted. First to make sure he didn't flip. Then to pick up his scent once he'd skipped. Ray was convinced you were the guy to flush out any plant. He died about a month ago. I waited a couple of weeks, then sent out the e-mail hiring you."

"And the texts?"

"It was critical that you harass Beacon. Keep 'em off balance and lure them out. I thought the texts might help things along. Honestly, it was the same idea behind having Ray's body surface in the Ambassador. Just gave Beacon something else to think about."

"So I was the bait, and Karen Simone took it."

"Her background always bothered me. When she showed an interest in you, it got my attention. We broke her cover late this afternoon. I put a guy on your tail and, sure enough, she made a move."

Karen flashed through my mind a final time—her face in the striped moonlight, hands locked together, gripping the bone-white handle of a .22-caliber pistol.

"Are you still following Ray's plan?" I said.

"Ray was a good friend. So, yeah, I'm following the plan."

"What's next?"

"You put the gun in the backseat."

I slipped it under the tarp alongside the rifle.

"And the one you have in your pocket."

I took out the other gun and put it in the back. "Pretty good, Wallace."

"Thank you. And I appreciate it."

"Now what?"

Wallace pulled out a smartphone and hit a few buttons. "I'm transferring a hundred thousand dollars into your account."

"Keep it."

"Marie wants you to have it." Wallace finished tapping on the phone and snapped it shut. "That's it. Your part in this is finished."

"Just like that?"

"Why not?"

I held up my bandaged hand. "For one thing, someone took a piece of my finger. I'd like to get a little payback. And then there's Marie."

"What about her?"

"Why is she driving out to the suburbs with a bag full of cash?"

Wallace paled a bit around the edges but quickly recovered. "Let it go, Michael."

"I know about the highway accidents Beacon caused. What I figure is she's trying to make things right with the victims by giving them some of the money. Maybe you agree with the idea. Maybe you don't. What I don't understand is why she has to deliver it herself."

"That's a personal decision."

"Know what I think?"

"I don't care."

"I think she might be playing both sides of this. Her dead husband and her father."

"How do you figure that?"

"Marie could be paying those victims because it's the right thing to do. Or she could be working with her old man and paying them off to keep *quiet* about Beacon. Or she could just be in it for herself."

"Marie was in this with Ray."

"And now Ray's conveniently dead. What if I told you Marie met with her father earlier today? Right after her trip to the suburbs?"

Wallace didn't respond, but I could see the meeting with Bones had caught him off guard.

"Think it through, Wallace. If I'm right, you'd be the next logical candidate to go."

"Where do you want me to drop you off?"

"You trust that family?"

"I trusted Ray. And I trust his wife. Most of all, I trust the money. And only I know exactly where it is. Now, where do you want to go?"

CHAPTER 39

Wallace dropped me in front of the Hancock Building. I leaned through the window for a final word. "Think about what I told you."

"Marie's disappearing tonight, Michael. With the money. Do yourself a favor and move on."

"She's got something else going on. Something neither of us knows about."

"Your cash is in the account. Take a trip somewhere. You deserve it."

Wallace rolled up the window. I watched him drive off, then walked east until I hit inner Lake Shore Drive. The sun was just lifting from the horizon, spilling a paint bucket full of pinks and purples across the corrugated surface of the lake. If I could have kept my eyes open, I might have felt inspired. As it was, I turned my back on the day and trudged back up Walton Place to the Knickerbocker Hotel. The receptionist didn't give me a second look. Checking in at dawn apparently wasn't that unusual at the Knickerbocker. I got a room on the fourth floor, put out the DO NOT DISTURB sign, and crawled into bed.

Nine hours later, I woke up and stared at three tiny cracks in the hotel ceiling. It was a little after two in the afternoon, and I wondered who was looking for me. I powered up my phone and checked my messages. My dog walker had fed Mags and taken her out. That was it. I sent the walker a text asking if she could take Mags for the night. Then I got out of bed and stumbled over to the windows. The shades were dark green and pulled down tight. I lifted one and stared out at the façade of the Drake Hotel. Below me traffic honked its way up the street. I turned from the windows, rubbed my face, and noticed a cream-colored envelope slipped under the door.

Michael,

I'm sorry how things turned out. Andrew said you had a lot of questions. Unfortunately, the answers aren't always as clear as we'd like. By the time you read this, I hope to be gone from the city for good. Please don't try to follow. Andrew and I have plans for the money. Good plans. I get the feeling you don't believe me. I guess I can't blame you, but it's just how things have to be. As for Beacon—leave them alone, and they'll leave you alone. I'm afraid that's the best I can do. Andrew has sent along details on the wire transfer in a separate e-mail. Please take the money and enjoy it.

Godspeed,
Marie

I stuck the note back in its envelope and went into the bathroom where I took a shower with my left hand hanging outside the curtain. Then I got dressed.

The hallway on the fourth floor of the Knickerbocker was empty. I took the elevator downstairs, strolled through the lobby, and out onto the sidewalk. I could have headed over to Marie Perry's apartment and seen if she was still in town. I could have called Vince Rodriguez and tried to convince him to start arresting people. Or I could have gone to the bank and counted my money. My feet didn't like any of those options, and I found myself walking down Huron Street. I stopped in front of Prentice Hospital and watched the cars come and go. Everyone in a hurry. I pushed through the revolving doors and went inside.

The tenth floor was deserted. I walked down the hall, past the NICU, to the Safe Haven office. The nurse at the front recognized me and buzzed me into the nursery. I gave her a wave and headed toward Vince's pod. I had a feeling about what I might find when I got there, and I wasn't wrong. The machines perched like dark angels around his empty crib. The menagerie of toys I'd brought was gone. I reached down into the trash and found the Post-it with Vince's name on it. I smoothed it out, folded it up, and stuck it in my pocket. Then I sat in the chair I usually sat in and stared at the spot where the kid used to be, my eyes hunting for the outline of his body in the fresh bedding. But there was nothing there. Just another bed waiting for the next throwaway child. And a reminder I'd leave no footprints in the sand save my own.

Soft voices filtered in from the other end of the nursery. It sounded like the singsong drone of a prayer, and I walked toward it. A green curtain was half drawn. Inside four people held hands in a circle and chained together a litany of Hail Marys. As I approached, the circle opened to reveal an old man in the center. He cradled a naked baby in the enormous palm of one hand and kissed its forehead through the dying words of an Our Father. The man's face was cut from the stony cliffs of Connemara or Mayo. His hair was pure white; his eyes, liquid pools of grief. For just a moment, I was drowning in them. Then someone tugged at my shoulder and snapped the curtain shut. I turned to find Amanda Mason staring at me.

"What are you doing?" she whispered.

"I came to see Vince."

"He's gone."

"I know." I looked back at the curtain. The prayers continued behind it, voices rising and falling in a hypnotic rhythm.

"Their child just passed," Amanda said. "We're giving the family a moment."

"Yeah."

"Are you all right?"

I nodded. I'd seen a lot of death. Hell, I'd shot someone dead the night before. But I'd never felt anything quite like that. The limp, naked child. The circle of prayer. The man. His hands, thick and horned. His face.

"I'm fine, Amanda. Sorry, I didn't realize . . ."

"They took Vince yesterday. I was going to call you, but I didn't have a number."

She had my number, but it didn't really matter.

"Where is he?"

"He'll be placed in a state-supervised facility until they find a permanent home." Amanda's voice had beaten a strategic retreat behind the high wall of hospital bureaucracy. I couldn't half blame her.

"Thanks," I said.

She touched the back of my hand. "He'll be fine, Michael."

"I know. I gotta run."

"You sure you're all right?"

"I'm good."

I wasn't good. Far from it. The hospital's chapel was on the second floor. I found a bench at the back and wove together a couple more Hail Marys. My thoughts circled back to the kid I'd named Vince. I'd done little more than sit in a nursery, smile into his eyes, and watch his heartbeat on a screen. A handful of moments. And yet the emptiness ate at me. The vulnerability shook me. I thought about the little family I'd stumbled on. The old man's cupped palm, a child in its very center, limbs lifeless and dangling. I opened my eyes and sat up straight in the pew, thoughts and prayers scattering like so many marbles, rolling to and fro across the shiny wooden floor. An image formed in my mind, a picture. One I'd seen at least twice. And never understood until now.

CHAPTER 40

I sat in my office and poured myself a short glass of whiskey. At my elbow were the file folders I'd unearthed from the bottom of Ray Perry's trunk. I opened one and found Ray's birth certificate, his marriage certificate, and a diploma from Northwestern Law School. Underneath the diploma was Ray's will. I picked up the thick document in one hand and considered its weight. Then I set it aside with everything else. At the bottom of the pile, I found the folder I was looking for, baby blue and faded with age. Clipped to the cover was the picture I'd first seen framed on Ray's old desk. The former governor was caught in a bloom of light, his head bent over an infant. The child was wrapped in a blanket, one arm flung awkwardly toward the camera. I took a slug of whiskey and studied the photo. Then I thought about the old man at Prentice. And the dead child he'd held in his hand. I looked at the picture of Ray again, the splay of the child's limbs, and saw what I instinctively knew to be true. When death touched a body, it left its fingerprints. Even on an infant. The child Ray

Perry was holding was dead. And I needed to know why. I opened the folder and began to read.

The first item was an admission report from Northwestern Memorial Hospital, dated June 8, 2004. The patient's name was Marie Anne Perry. She was thirty-eight years old, eight months pregnant, and in labor. I flipped to the next page. At 2:32 p.m., she gave birth to a girl, weighing five pounds, three ounces. There was a lot of medical shorthand, but I got the sense the birth was considered a high-risk proposition. The last three pages, written in neat, uniform cursive, explained why. The girl had been born with a form of spina bifida. She was immediately taken from her mother and put into Northwestern's NICU. There seemed to be some possibility of surgery on the infant, but it was unclear if or when that was going to happen. The mother was doing well. The prognosis for the infant was guarded. Underneath the initial hospital reports I found two certificates clipped together. The first was a birth certificate for Emma Marie Perry, dated June 8, 2004. The second was the child's death certificate. Emma died from "respiratory complications" a day after she was born, on the afternoon of June 9.

I drank some more whiskey and thought about the lines carved into Marie Perry's face, the dry grief in her smile, the hole in her heart. I'd been wrong about Marie. And her secret. Still, it didn't make sense. Not the way it needed to. I flipped back to the hospital admission report and began to read, looking for the missing piece. At the bottom of the first page I found it—in the form of a street address.

CHAPTER 41

I cracked the window in my car and studied the unremarkable exterior of 254 Old Harbor Road. I now knew who lived inside. And why Marie Perry had shown up here yesterday.

Late-afternoon sun glinted off living room windows and car windshields up and down the block. A woman carrying a bag of groceries walked through a fracture of light and into a valley of shadow. It was the person I'd been waiting for. The person who didn't have her name on the deed but nonetheless lived at 254 Old Harbor. I waited until she was halfway up the front stairs before getting out of the car. She was just pulling out her keys as I hit the first step. Amanda Mason turned. "Mr. Kelly."

"Hi, Amanda."

Her eyes darted up and down the street, then behind her to make sure the front door was still closed. "You startled me."

"Sorry."

"What are you doing out here?"

"I think we need to talk."

"About what?" Her voice sounded hollow, like a pill rolling around inside an empty bottle.

"Might be better inside, Amanda."

"This is my home, Mr. Kelly. I have two children inside."

"I'm not going to harm your children."

"I didn't say you were, but I don't want them exposed . . . It doesn't matter. It's my home. If you want to talk, we can do it right here." The nurse stiffened her jaw and clutched the bag of groceries to her chest.

"It's about Emma Perry," I said and took out the hospital report from 2004. At the very bottom was Amanda Mason's name and address. Underneath that, her signature.

"You were the attending nurse, Amanda. I'd like to know what happened."

We sat at her kitchen table. I'd gotten a quick glimpse of her two girls before Amanda hustled them upstairs. One looked like a teenager, thick limbed with pale skin and straight auburn hair. The other was maybe nine or ten, with blue eyes and blond hair that ran halfway down her back. Amanda closed the kitchen door behind them and filled a kettle with water.

"You want some tea?"

"Sure." I watched her bustle back and forth with mugs and milk. Sugar, spoons, and tea bags. She waited by the stove, staring blankly out the window while the water came to a boil. Then she poured the tea and sat down. I fixed mine up with some milk and sugar and took a sip. Amanda pulled the admission report close and touched her signature on the bottom of the page. I'd attached Emma Perry's birth and death certificates.

"Where did you get all of this?" she said.

"Does it matter?"

"It might."

"I'm a private investigator. Ray Perry had it stashed among his personal belongings."

"Ray." Amanda sighed, and I thought the old nurse and charismatic governor might have been allies at some point, maybe even friends. Not that it mattered now.

"Does Marie know you have it?" she said, holding up the admission report with two fingers before dropping it back on the table.

"No."

"What is it you want?"

"I want the rest of the story."

"No, you don't."

"Try me."

Amanda stared at me as if I were suddenly made of wood, then fortified herself with a sip of tea. "What do you know about spina bifida?"

"Nothing."

"It's a congenital birth defect caused by an incomplete closing of the neural tube that houses the spine. There are different levels of severity. Mild cases can sometimes be corrected with surgery, and the child can still lead a fairly normal life. In severe cases the life expectancy is often three to four years. Sometimes less."

"I assume Emma had a severe form?"

"You saw the death certificate. She passed away a day after being born."

The child's passing sat with us for a moment. Amanda sipped some more tea and avoided my eyes.

"Why did Marie Perry come out here yesterday?" I said.

"Out here?"

I took out my phone and showed her the photo I'd taken of Marie at the front door to 254 Old Harbor. Amanda's face flushed with anger. "You like to spy on people, Mr. Kelly?"

"What I don't like is when people lie to me."

"I have no reason to lie."

"Sure you do. And you're not very good at it. If you help me, I'll try to protect whatever it is you want protected. If you don't, I'll leave here owing you nothing. And that's probably not the best spot for you to be in."

She played with a spoon on the table. Then she picked up the hospital report and read through it again. Finally, she stood up. "Can you wait here a moment?"

"Sure."

I could hear her walking through the house, then the opening and closing of a door. The house went still. No sound from Amanda. Nothing from the girls upstairs. Ten minutes passed, twenty. Finally, I heard footsteps returning. Amanda walked into the kitchen. She was alone. Her hands were empty.

"I'm sorry for making you wait." Her voice was hushed, almost afraid of itself.

"Not a problem. You want to sit down?"

"I don't think so."

"Why not?"

"You need to come with me, Mr. Kelly."

"Where are we going?"

"Just come with me."

I got up and followed Amanda into the bowels of the house.

CHAPTER 42

She walked me through a tidy living room to a door at the end of a hallway. The door opened to a set of steep stairs that ended in a finished basement. Amanda went to a second door and opened it. Inside was a dimly lit room finished in thin wood paneling and wall-to-wall carpeting. It might have once been intended as a family room, but now it served as a hospital ward. The patient was laid up in the far corner. He had tubes running into both arms and one up his nose. The machines that surrounded him kept time with the ragged rhythms of the patient's heart and lungs. Amanda walked me to the foot of the bed.

"This is my husband, Nicholas. Nicholas, this is Mr. Kelly."

Nicholas Mason had the sheets pulled up to his chest. He carried a few wisps of hair on his head and the scalp underneath looked crumbling and gray. His forehead overhung black eyes sunk deep into his skull and yellow bags of skin dripped off his cheekbones. I wasn't a doctor, but I knew death when it was in the room. And it was here. Grinning and licking its chops. Nicholas Mason waved off his wife.

"I'm fine, Amanda."

"I think I should stay." Her eyes flicked from me to her husband.

"Go," Mason said softly. "I'll buzz you when we're done."

Amanda closed the door behind her. I had the feeling she hadn't gone too far. Mason pointed to an empty chair.

"Sit if you want."

I took a seat. Nicholas Mason looked at me like he expected a question, but I didn't have anything for him. The dying man began to cough, a thick, muddy sound I could almost touch. He took a tissue from a table beside the bed and spit into it, then wadded it up and tucked it into his fist.

"I'd ask you to use that gun on me, but I'm not sure I'm worth the bullet."

"Why am I here, Mr. Mason?"

"Did my wife tell you what I did for a living?"

"No, she didn't."

"I was a hospital attendant at Prentice. That's how we met."

"Okay."

"There's a laptop on the other side of the bed. Maybe you could get it?"

I found the laptop and set it up on a small foldout table they used for Mason's meals. "Now what?"

He reached under his sheets and pulled out a black flash drive. "Play this."

I plugged in the flash drive and clicked on a video file. The screen filled with the image of a darkened hospital room. There was a white crib in the center of the room. A figure approached the crib and leaned over it.

"Stop the video," Mason said. I did.

"This was shot on the afternoon of June 9, 2004. The day

Emma Perry died. The person you see there is me. I'm putting a small pillow over the child's face in an effort to suffocate her."

I stared at the grainy image as Mason continued.

"I was paid to do it. Paid by someone who thought a special-needs child would derail Ray Perry's budding political career." Mason began to cough again, the sound rich and moist in his lungs. There was a glass of water by the bed. He took a long sip and leaned back on the starched pillows. "The thought was that the child would become Ray Perry's life and his prison, even if she only lived a few years. He'd delay his run for governor, and the window would slam shut. Chicago couldn't live with that. Ray was gonna run. One way or another."

"Who hired you?" I said.

"Who hired me?" Nicholas gave me a cracked grin. "Good question. Maybe it was Ray himself? Maybe the child's mother? I can see you don't believe that, but there's a hard streak in that family. Still, we're getting ahead of ourselves. Finish the tape."

There wasn't much more to see. The person stayed bent over the crib for a minute, maybe two. Then he stood up and left. "Stop the video, Mr. Kelly."

I did.

"Murder, correct?"

"Maybe."

Mason's fingers had dipped below his sheets. I touched my gun in its holster. "Why don't you keep your hands where I can see them?"

He showed me a mouth full of worm's teeth sunken into black gums. "I've got days, Mr. Kelly. Maybe hours. So let's not waste time with foolishness. The tape you watched is a fraud. At least it is if you think you've just watched a murder."

"Go ahead."

"Yes, that's me on the tape. And yes, I was hired to kill Emma Perry."

"Why you?"

"I had a criminal record before I came to work at Prentice. I'd lied about it, but certain people in Chicago have a way of ferreting those things out. I assume that's why I was approached."

"Makes sense."

"I wanted to go to the cops, but my wife had a different idea."

"And what was that?"

"I wanted to save the child." Amanda Mason had slipped back into the room and was standing just behind me. "I didn't think the police would believe us. And I didn't think Emma would ever be safe. Not in that family. We argued about it, but I finally convinced Nicholas to *pretend* to kill the baby."

"What about the documents? The death certificate?"

"We phonied it all up," Amanda said. "I was running the NICU. It wasn't that hard."

"I saw a picture of Ray Perry holding a dead child."

"We're not proud of that," Amanda said.

"The hell we're not." Mason gripped the rails that ran along either side of his bed and pulled himself upright. The effort it took was terrifying. "We used an infant who'd passed away. An orphan. We wrapped the child up and let the Perrys hold it. Let them think it was Emma."

"So Ray and Marie didn't hire you?"

"It was Bones McIntyre," Mason said, letting the name drip off his lips and nodding at the frozen image on screen. "He hired me and then hid a video camera in the child's room. I knew about the camera and had a pretty good idea he'd use the tape at some point. An insurance policy to make sure I kept my mouth shut. I was right."

"And you let him think he got away with it?"

"We did it to protect Emma," Amanda said. "As long as everyone thought she was dead, she'd be safe."

"But she's not dead."

Amanda shook her head.

"Then where is she?" I said, already knowing the answer.

Amanda gave her husband a shot of something to put him to sleep and covered him with blankets. Then we went back upstairs and had a second cup of tea.

"Emma was the blond-haired girl I saw when I came in," I said.

Amanda nodded. "I thought there'd be questions, but no one batted an eye. Of course, we're a quiet couple. Not a lot of friends. I think that helped."

"When did you tell Marie her daughter was alive?"

"Just after Ray disappeared. I wanted to do it sooner, but Nicholas wasn't sure. He still thought Ray might have been involved in the plan to kill Emma and didn't want to risk it."

"What was Marie's reaction when you told her?"

"Hysterical. Didn't believe it. Then she met Emma and knew. She wanted to move the girl, but decided to keep her here. It was close enough where Marie could visit and it was safe."

"And it's the only home her daughter's ever known."

"The long-term plan has always been to get them both out of Chicago."

"But Bones has been watching his daughter?"

"Her greatest fear is that he finds out Emma's alive."

"Tell me about her."

For the first time, the nurse's composure cracked. I heard it in the seams between her words. "Emma's a gift."

"I bet."

"Her form of spina bifida turned out to be not as bad as

everyone originally feared. We took her out of state for an operation right after she was born. She got rid of the walker a year and a half ago and is expected to lead a normal life."

"That's a wonderful thing, Amanda."

"Yes, it is." She dropped her head in her hands and wept. It was a desperate sound only a mother could make. "I did the best I could, Mr. Kelly. Took her to a clinic in St. Louis so as to avoid any attention. Loved her every bit as much as my own. Maybe more."

Outside a spring rain began to fall, sudden and hard against the roof. Amanda wiped her nose and looked out the window like she'd never seen a storm before. "It wasn't supposed to rain tonight."

"Weathermen never know what they're talking about."

She sniffed at the obvious truth.

"Emma can't stay here forever," I said.

"She won't."

I could sense another shift, the widening distance in her voice telling me I was still on the outside. Neither parent, nor protector, nor anything close. So I asked another question I already knew the answer to. "Where is she, Amanda?"

"She's already gone, Mr. Kelly. Gone with her mother and never coming back."

CHAPTER 43

It took me three days to find mother and daughter. Another three to convince the mother to see me. We met in my living room. I'd had the apartment swept earlier that morning and all the bugs removed. Then I'd had it swept again. Marie Perry sat in a hard chair facing the street. She spoke without ever having been asked a question.

"The story I told you about me when I was seventeen."

"The abortion?"

"That was true. Afterward, the doctor insisted I could never have children. When I told Ray, it ruined him. Until, of course, I got pregnant."

"He wanted the child?"

"He lived for it. Then we got the diagnosis of spina bifida, and Ray wasn't so sure anymore. My father was adamant I have an abortion. He never knew about the first one—not that it would have mattered—but my father knew Ray. And he knew Ray wouldn't have the heart for politics once the child was born. Eventually, Ray came around to my father's way of thinking. He told me an abortion was 'the best thing for both of us.' "

"And what did you say?"

"I told him I'd rather die than give up our child. So I had the baby and killed our marriage instead." Marie closed her eyes and turned her face a degree toward the sun streaming through an open window. It seemed like a long time before she spoke again. "What do you know about spina bifida?"

"Amanda gave me the basics."

"It's interesting. You meet with the doctor every few weeks during your pregnancy. You look at the ultrasounds of your child and listen while they take things away. First, it's her ability to walk normally. Then it's her ability to walk at all. She'll likely be brain damaged, emotionally impaired, and live her life tethered to a colostomy bag. The defect is growing. The defect has stabilized. We just won't know until she's born, but it won't be good. It's never good. And all the while, people look at you like you're carrying an alien inside you and whisper in your ear about things like 'quality of life' and the 'right thing for the baby.' And then the child no one wants but you is born. And the knives come out for real."

"Was Ray involved with Emma after she was born?"

"You mean did he hire someone to kill his own daughter?" Marie shook her head. "Ray and I both thought Emma had died of natural causes. The whole thing was swept under the rug and never talked about again. My father had a campaign to run and a governor's mansion to win. Emma wasn't going to get in the way."

I thought about Iphigenia and the bleached sails of the Greeks as an army set sail for Troy. "Money, glory, and power."

Her smile sparked a million tiny bits of pain. "Seems like Euripides had it just about right."

"That's why he's Euripides."

"I guess."

"Tell me about Beacon Limited."

"What's to tell? My father *is* Beacon. Always has been. He brought Ray in once we got to Springfield."

"Why did Ray disappear with Beacon's money?"

"He didn't want to go to jail. And he was greedy. I helped because I didn't want him in my life anymore, even from a prison cell."

"Did Ray think you'd eventually join him?"

"Ray thought a lot of things, most of it dictated by his ego. That was Ray, for better or worse. Once I found out Emma was still alive, she became my only priority. And Ray became a possible way out. Or so I'd hoped."

"When did Ray discover his daughter was alive?"

"He saw a picture before he died. That was all he deserved." Outside the sun dipped behind some cloud cover, burying her face in deep shadow. "Ray used people, Mr. Kelly. He used me to further his career, then to help him get out of the courthouse. Andrew Wallace did a hundred things for Ray, including stealing sixty million dollars from Beacon. You were Ray's final stalking horse—someone who would smoke out any threats planted in our midst."

"You mean Karen Simone?"

"I wouldn't have guessed her, but, yes, Karen Simone. That was your job. And you were well paid for it. Now that she's dead, maybe there's a window. A chance to get away. If so, I intend to use it."

"Your father will hunt you down, Marie. The man wants his money. And you're his only lead."

"I have a plan."

"You mean the church?"

The question hung like a dagger between us. Marie reached for it. "What do you know about that?"

"I know you met your father there. I'm guessing it had

something to do with the money you drove out to Clarendon Hills and Hinsdale."

"I gave him sworn statements from two families. Both will testify that Beacon Limited killed their loved ones."

"More blackmail?"

"I want my father focused on me. Believing I'm a viable threat to him and his pals."

"Meanwhile, Amanda gets your daughter out of town, and Wallace arranges it so the cash follows."

"The original plan was for both of us to go, but that might not happen. The important thing is that my father never know Emma's alive. I'll stay here and distract him by threatening to take the lid off Beacon."

"Your plaintiffs will be paid off, Marie. Count on it."

"I don't think so."

"They took your money to speak up. They'll take more from Beacon to keep quiet. Your father understands that. In some ways, that's his greatest strength. And biggest weakness."

"Money?"

"Greed. All you have to do is exploit it. Tell him the truth. You have the cash Ray stole. And you're willing to bargain for your freedom."

"Why should I trust him?"

"Wallace and I have worked it out so you don't have to."

She didn't know Wallace and I had been talking. It threw her for a minute. "How?"

"We set aside ten million for you and Emma. Another ten gets split between the families. The rest is funneled back to Beacon over a period of years. Gives you time to disappear and lets the wounds heal."

"The wounds will never heal."

"Maybe not. But if you go ahead with your plan, they'll blow it out of the water, and then they'll kill you. When they find out Emma is alive, they'll kill her as well. Or maybe Bones takes custody and raises her as his own."

A horn beeped somewhere, and a car door slammed. The sun peeked out again from its cloud cover, throwing shards of light across the room. Marie walked to the windows and studied the street below. "I made the decision to have an abortion when I was seventeen. Then I fought to save my baby when I was thirty-eight. At the time I felt each decision was the right one. Now I feel like I've only created a culture of death."

"That's one way to think about it."

Marie turned from the window. "You have another?"

"There probably would have been suffering however you chose. It's what you do afterward that counts. What lives you protect. How well you persevere."

She crossed her arms and leaned up against the windowsill. "Will I have to tell him about Emma?"

"It's the only way."

"Why?"

Marie listened as I laid out the deal I hoped to strike with her father.

"Is that all of it?"

"That's all you need to know."

"And I trust you for the rest?"

"Your little girl will be safe. I can promise you that."

"And it will be over?"

"It should be, yes."

"I hope you're right, Mr. Kelly." She turned away from me again. "Go ahead and make the call."

CHAPTER 44

Spyder nudged the suppressor another inch outside the window and nestled his cheek against the smooth stock of the rifle. The woman was little more than a shadow, loitering too far from the open window to get a fix on. Kelly was a couple of feet to her left and every bit as elusive. Spyder moved his scope over to a bird, hopping from branch to branch on a nearby tree. He adjusted the sights and painted a crosshair across the bird's back. Then he slipped a finger inside the trigger guard and squeezed, slow and easy. The bird flew off in a burst of feathers just as the hammer snapped forward on an empty chamber.

"Fuck." Spyder pulled back from the window and laid the rifle on the floor. It was warm in the apartment. Spyder stripped off his gloves and took a sip of Gatorade. The flat was empty, save for the rifle, its case, and a plastic bag filled with trash. Spyder had packed up all the gear last night and spent the morning washing the place down with hot water and bleach. He was more than ready for the job to be done. And was looking forward to collecting his bonus. A floorboard creaked somewhere in the apartment; a hot breeze rustled the curtains behind him. Spyder took another sip of Gatorade and looked across the street.

"Shit."

She was there, forehead pressed against the windowpane, staring down at the sidewalk. Spyder pulled on his gloves and picked up the rifle again. He wasn't afraid of being spotted. She could look right at him and see nothing but the black rectangle of a window. He rested the barrel on the sill and fixed his eye to the scope. He'd said he could take out both of them. His bosses knew better and put a man in a car downstairs. Spyder's priority was the woman. She moved a fraction in his sights. Spyder adjusted and sharpened his focus. The woman turned her back to him. Spyder tickled the sight up and down her spine. She drifted back into the shadows. Spyder withdrew the rifle. He loaded three rounds into the magazine and chambered the first. Then he leaned the rifle up against the wall. He took a picture of Marie Perry out of his pocket and compared it with the woman he'd seen at the window. She'd aged, and not well, but it was her. Spyder put the picture back in his pocket and closed his eyes. All he needed now was a phone call. And a clean shot.

CHAPTER 45

Bones McIntyre agreed to meet his daughter alone, with only myself acting as a go-between. I told him it had to happen this afternoon, or it wasn't going to happen at all. Bones balked at the timing, but the lure of the money was too strong. A little more than an hour later, a cab pulled up in front of my building, and the old man got out. He took his time walking up the three flights to my apartment. I waited on the landing.

"Hip doesn't like all the stairs."

"She's in the living room."

Bones grunted and moved past me, into the apartment. "How about a glass of water?"

I went out to the kitchen and filled a glass. When I returned Marie was staring at a window streaked with sunlight. Bones sat ten feet away, hands folded in his lap, studying his left shoe. I gave Bones his water and moved my chair so I was equidistant from both.

"You guys gonna talk to each other?"

"I thought that's what you were here for." Marie spoke without taking her eyes off the window.

"Where's the money your husband stole?" Bones took a sip of water and rubbed his lips together like it was a fine wine.

"We need assurances," I said.

"I already gave them over the phone."

I shook my head. "I told you that wasn't enough."

"You told me I'd have the money in return for allowing my daughter and her felon of a husband to escape criminal prosecution and disappear for good."

"Ray's dead," Marie said, her voice like fallen leaves stirring in the gutter.

"Good riddance." Bones crossed himself and took another sip of water. "We knew about it the day he turned up at the Ambassador. I assume you had the good sense to secure the cash?"

"She did," I said.

"Of course she did. She's my daughter."

"You sicken me," Marie said.

"And yet here you sit." Bones turned to me. "What do you want out of this?"

"The truth."

"In Chicago? That's easy. Pick one out and I'll tell you a bedtime story."

"Let's start with Eddie Ward and Paul Goggin. A couple of guys who helped Ray Perry escape from the federal courthouse two years ago. You knew about them and watched them. Ultimately, you decided they didn't know a thing about Ray's whereabouts or the money, so you killed them. To send a message maybe to the people who did."

"I'm not sure I like your story," Bones said. "Hopefully you've got the ending right."

"You were never sure what your daughter knew. And proceeded with caution. Smart move there, Bones. But the bodies started things rolling. Then Ray himself turns up dead, and Marie is all that's left. Maybe she knows where the money is? But if she did, why didn't she disappear with her husband? And what are you gonna do about it anyway? Kill your own flesh and blood? I'd think it might be pretty hard to live with something like that, but I've been wrong before." I took out the black flash drive Nicholas Mason had given me and put it on the table. "Which brings us to this."

"What's that?" Bones said.

"Seven days ago, a man named Nicholas Mason gave it to me."

The old man's nostrils flared. "Never heard of him."

"In 2004, Nicholas worked as an attendant in the hospital where your daughter had a baby girl."

"That's family business. And it was a long time ago."

"Yeah, well, the video's still pretty good. It shows Mason suffocating the child in her crib."

Bones wet his lips. When he spoke, his teeth glittered like polished pearls. "What's any of that got to do with me?"

"Mason died two days ago. Before he passed, he appeared in a second video." I took out another flash drive and set it beside the first. "In it, he went into great detail explaining how you hired him to kill the child. He even tape recorded a conversation he had with you." I tapped the second drive. "All right here."

Bones took a gun out of his pocket and pointed it at his daughter. "I did what needed to be done. What no one else had the stomach for."

Marie still hadn't looked at her father. I took out my own gun and leveled it at his belly.

"Put it away, Bones."

"If I'm gonna get shot, I'd rather it be with something in my hand."

"I could have put a bullet in you ten minutes ago if I'd wanted. Put the gun down."

"After you."

I lowered my gun and placed it on the table. Bones did the same. My smartphone was in my pocket and buzzed with a text. Everyone in the room ignored it.

"We're not here to settle old scores," I said. "We just want you to know what we have. And what we'll hang on to."

"So you're blackmailing me?"

"I can't tie you to Ward or Goggin. This way everyone feels comfortable with the arrangement going forward."

"Where's the money?"

I took out a slip of paper and pushed it across the table. "The accounts are numbered and will be set up in whatever names you want. Marie keeps ten for herself and ten for the families. You get twenty today. The rest will be paid out over three years, provided Marie's safe."

Bones took a look at the paper I'd given him, folded it in half and put it in his pocket. "And how do I know she'll keep her end of the bargain once we leave here?"

"Two reasons," I said and held up two fingers. "First of all, there's me."

"You?"

"I live in Chicago and I'm not going anywhere. If she reneges, my life is forfeit. You know your daughter. Do you think she'd let me die?"

Bones thought about that, then nodded. "What's the other reason?"

I glanced at Marie who turned in her chair and leaned toward her father. For a moment I thought she was going to go after him, teeth and claws bared. Instead, she just hung there, their knees and faces inches apart.

"The other reason's sitting outside, Father."

"Outside?" Bones gave me a quick, almost frantic look, but his daughter demanded his attention.

"Nicholas Mason lied to you. He never killed anyone. He and his wife took my baby and kept her safe until they could figure out who in our family could be trusted. Her name is Emma. She's ten years old, she's healthy, and she's your granddaughter."

I watched Bones's face turn to melted rubber. His lips stretched and moved, but no sound came out.

"That's the other reason you can rest assured I'll keep my end of the bargain. I'm a mother. And I'll do whatever it takes to keep my child as far away from you as possible."

"I don't believe it."

A ghost of a smile played across Marie Perry's lips. "I'm going to give you a gift. I'm going to let you see your granddaughter. For the last time in your life." She nodded toward the open windows. "She's in a cab out front."

We both watched as Bones McIntyre got up from his seat and shuffled to the windows. He leaned out and looked down into the street. Amanda Mason got out of a yellow cab with a blond-haired girl wearing a light blue dress. The girl looked up, one hand shading her face. Amanda let the moment sit for a heartbeat, then folded Emma back into the cab. Bones pressed his head against the windowsill and closed his eyes. I wondered what the old man was thinking about. His money. His daughter. His granddaughter. I wondered where ambition ended and evil began, and if anyone had ever charted that border on a map. Bones opened his eyes and turned back toward Marie. A pane of glass shattered as the sniper's bullet struck him in the back of the neck with a quiet thump. Bones fell gracelessly at his daughter's feet. His hand scratched once on the wooden floor. Then Bones McIntyre was dead.

CHAPTER 46

Marie stared dryly at her father's body. "Was that the rest of your plan?"

"He never would have let it go," I said. "You and Emma never would have been safe."

She looked up. "And you think we'll be safe now?"

"With your father dead, there's a chance. Come on."

I pulled her from the chair and led her back into the kitchen.

"Who shot him?" she said.

"Bones had a man planted across the street, watching this apartment. My guess is they were going to try to kill us both once your father got his money. Wallace took out their man while we talked to Bones. When Andrew was ready, he texted me."

"Andrew shot my father?"

"He agreed it was the only way to keep you safe. All we had to do was get your father to the windows. I figured a chance to glimpse his granddaughter might do it."

My phone buzzed with another text. I pulled out the phone and read it. Then I went back into the living room and picked up my gun off the table.

"Where's Emma?" Marie said, her voice rising.

"Andrew's headed down to the street right now. He'll make sure she's all right." I walked to the front door and checked the lock. Marie followed in my wake.

"What's wrong?"

"Nothing. Andrew just thinks there might be a second gun . . ."

"Emma." Marie slipped the lock and bolted down the stairs. She hit the lobby ten seconds later and swung into the street. I was a half step behind her. The first slug tore a good chunk of wood off the door frame. I dove back into the doorway. Three more shots stitched me into a corner. Marie was crouched behind a Volvo. The gunman was almost directly across the street and moving to get a better angle on me. He'd have it in a matter of seconds. I rolled onto the sidewalk and came up against the side of an SUV. Iron Belly flashed between two cars, gun up, looking for me in the empty doorway. When he realized his mistake, he turned and fired two wild shots, shattering a windshield behind me. I drilled him twice in the stomach and watched him fall into a flower bed. Then I turned and looked for Marie.

I found her slumped against the front bumper of a rusted-out Toyota, arms awkwardly by her side, eyes open and full of sky. Best I could tell, one of Iron Belly's rounds had come up off the pavement and caught her in the cheek. I figured she was dead before she hit the ground. My phone buzzed again in my pocket. It was Wallace. He had Emma and Amanda with him. The girl wanted to see her mother. I texted back and told him to wait. Then I closed Marie Perry's eyes and carried her into my building.

CHAPTER 47

Chicago PD blocked off the street and pulled Iron Belly's body out of the flower bed. By the time Rodriguez showed up, they'd found the other shooter in an apartment across the street. Andrew Wallace had put a .22 slug in his head and planted the weapon in Iron Belly's car.

"So this needs to go down as a gunfight between the guy in the street and the guy in the apartment?" Rodriguez was sitting in my kitchen, sipping coffee from a Styrofoam cup and not believing a word of what he was saying.

"Will it work?" I said.

"Except for the fact that the weapons and angles are all wrong, sure. What about Marie Perry?"

I'd laid her out on the cool wood floor of my living room and sat with her until the police came. Then I'd watched, carving her features into my brain while they took their pictures and zipped up the coroner's bag. No one said a word as they loaded her onto a stretcher and wheeled her to a van waiting in the alley.

"She was caught in the crossfire," I said.

"Shit."

"Have the coroner hold a press conference and announce that Ray's dead. Leak Marie's death as a suspected suicide a couple of days later. She wouldn't care."

Rodriguez walked to the front windows of my apartment and looked out. Down the block, a handful of residents and a couple of news crews had gathered behind the yellow police tape. "What about the press?"

"It'll be a story tomorrow. Then Beacon will muzzle them. Trust me, they're not gonna want anyone taking too close a look at any of this."

"And when does someone come looking for you?"

"The whole thing dies with Marie and Ray."

"Bones won't let it go."

"He's dead, too."

"Course he is."

"You want to hear about it?"

"I guess I better."

So I sat down at the table and talked. About the sixty million Ray skimmed. About his wife helping him disappear. About the little girl they had ten years ago. About her grandfather who hired a man to kill her. When I'd finished, Rodriguez just shook his head.

"Where's the girl now?" he said.

"Safe with the woman who brought her up."

"Does the girl know about her mom?"

"Not yet."

"And you really think Beacon's just gonna wash their hands of this?"

"Marie's dead. Ray's dead. Bones is dead. I'm guessing they write off the money and move on."

Rodriguez sighed and got up from the table.

"Roderick Hampton," I said.

"He's already out. All the charges were dropped."

"And Eddie Ward?"

"I took a quick look at the piece the guy in the street had on him when he went into the flower bed. Same caliber. Same brand of bullet. I'll run a ballistics check tomorrow."

"Good."

"You gonna see the Perry girl again?"

"Tomorrow morning."

"Tell whoever has her to get her out of the city. And make sure Bones stays put. Wherever he is."

CHAPTER 48

I met Andrew Wallace the next morning at the Golden Nugget on Diversey. He'd driven all night with Bones McIntyre's body in his trunk. Now the trunk was empty, and Bones was planted at the bottom of a freshly poured concrete footing for a bridge in Indiana. Seemed just about right.

"Where's Amanda?" I said.

"She's gonna meet me here."

"Is she okay with this?"

Wallace had ordered a stack of pancakes and smeared butter and syrup on them. "Why not? She loves the girl and her husband's dead. Nothing to keep her here."

"Where will they go?"

Wallace cut into the stack and shook his head as he chewed. "Probably better if you don't know."

He was right.

"How about you?" I said.

"I'll get them situated, then I'm done."

"And the money?"

Wallace poured a little more syrup over his cakes. "I've got it somewhere safe. When the time's right, I'll spread it out, move it around, and eventually circle it back to the girl."

"Nothing for you?"

"Amanda wanted me to take five."

"Leaving fifty-five for the girl?"

"Amanda wants to funnel a good chunk of it to the families of the accident victims, as well as a few charities Marie had identified. But the girl will never want. That's for sure." Wallace looked out the window. A Checker cab was pulling into the lot. "That's them. I know we talked about this, but Amanda wants you to take a cut."

I shook my head. "I've already gotten more than I wanted from this job."

"You sure? It's a lot of money. A life-changer."

Outside Amanda Mason was paying the cabbie. Then she and her two girls were standing in the lot, blinking against the morning sun.

"I'm sure." I pulled out a letter and pushed it across the table. "Tell Amanda to give this to Emma when she's old enough."

Wallace picked up the envelope. "What is it?"

"Just a letter. Telling her about her mom."

Wallace stuffed the envelope in his pocket and stood up. "You think they're gonna come after us?"

"Beacon?"

"Whoever. That's a lot of cash."

"You buried their last lead in Indiana. Besides, in Chicago there's always a new meal ticket getting punched. Onward and upward."

"You're probably right. Either way, I gotta scoot." Wallace stuck out his hand. "Marie was right. You're a good man."

"Thanks for the help, Andrew."

"I'll be seeing you. Not."

I watched him walk out into the sunshine. Amanda looked back at the restaurant, and for a moment I thought she might come in. But Wallace herded her and the girls to his car. They climbed in and drove away. I sipped at my coffee and pulled a second envelope out of my pocket. Inside was a flash drive with a couple of hours of video recorded in Rachel Swenson's apartment. Rodriguez had pulled the stuff off a computer they'd found in Bones's office. I wasn't sure if there were other copies, but we'd all have to take our chances. I pulled out my laptop, plugged in the flash drive, and deleted all the files. Then I pocketed the drive and called for the check. I was about to pay when my phone buzzed with an e-mail.

Mr. Kelly,

Andrew gave me your letter. I'll make sure Emma reads it when the time is right. And I'll make sure she knows about you as well. Last night I asked Andrew to set up an interest-bearing account for you and wire two million dollars into it. There's a secure link below and details on how to access the money. I know you don't want this, but I also know Marie would have wanted you to have it. So it's there, collecting interest, if you change your mind. Thank you for giving Emma a new life. Myself and my daughter as well. Please be safe.

Amanda

I reread the message. Then I accessed the account and looked at the outstanding balance. A lot of zeros. All of them drenched in blood. I finished my coffee, paid the bill, and left. On the way out, my phone sang again. Another e-mail. This one was from Elena Ramirez. She was going to have a baby girl. And she was going to name it Kelly.

Notes and Acknowledgments

As with all the Michael Kelly books, I've tried to be as accurate as possible when it comes to Chicago's geography, buildings, and institutions. Where necessary, however, I've taken certain liberties to fit the needs of the story. Sterch's, for example, was a real bar on Chicago's North Side. Unfortunately, it closed a few years back. I decided to resurrect it for *The Governor's Wife* mostly because Sterch's was Kelly's kind of place. And there aren't many bars like it left in Chicago—or anywhere else for that matter. If you want to read more about the place, check out the Chicago Bar Project, www.chibarproject.com.

I'd like to thank my editor, Jordan Pavlin; her boss, Sonny Mehta; and all the people at Knopf and Vintage/Black Lizard for their unwavering support of the Kelly books.

Thanks, also, to my agent, David Gernert; Chicago writer Garnett Kilberg Cohen; and my family and friends for all their support and encouragement. Special thanks to Chase Ehrenberg for her discerning editorial eye and wonderful way with words.

Thanks, finally, to everyone who has read my other novels. Hope you enjoy this one.

That's it. Love you, Mary Frances.

A NOTE ABOUT THE AUTHOR

Michael Harvey is the author of *The Chicago Way, The Fifth Floor, The Third Rail, We All Fall Down,* and *The Innocence Game,* as well as a journalist and documentary producer. His work has won numerous national and international awards, including multiple news Emmys, two Primetime Emmy nominations, and an Academy Award nomination. He holds a law degree with honors from Duke University, a master's degree in journalism from Northwestern University, and a bachelor's degree, magna cum laude, in classical languages from Holy Cross College. He lives, of course, in Chicago.

A NOTE ON THE TYPE

The text of this book was composed in Trump Mediæval. Designed by Professor Georg Trump (1896–1985) in the mid-1950s, Trump Mediæval was cut and cast by the C. E. Weber Type Foundry of Stuttgart, Germany. The roman letterforms are based on classical prototypes, but Professor Trump has imbued them with his own unmistakable style. The italic letterforms, unlike those of so many other typefaces, are closely related to their roman counterparts. The result is a truly contemporary type, notable for both its legibility and its versatility.

Typeset by Scribe, Philadelphia, Pennsylvania
Printed and bound by Berryville Graphics, Berryville, Virginia
Designed by Maggie Hinders